A Perilous Marriage

Marriage by Necessity: Book 1

A Perilous Marriage

Ruth Ann Nordin

This is a work of fiction. The events and characters described herein are imaginary and are not intended to refer to specific places or living persons. The opinions expressed in this manuscript are solely the opinions of the author and also represent the opinions or thoughts of the publisher.

A Perilous Marriage

V1.0
Cover images by Period Images and Dreamstime. Cover Text, Logo and Branding by Ruth Ann Nordin.

This book is dedicated to my good friend, Eris Hyrkas.
I’m blessed to have you in my life.

If you love Regencies, here are the ones Ruth has done so far. For a complete list of all of Ruth's books, go to the end of this book.

Marriage by Scandal Series
The Earl's Inconvenient Wife
A Most Unsuitable Earl
His Reluctant Lady
The Earl's Scandalous Wife

Marriage by Design Series
Breaking the Rules
Nobody's Fool
A Deceptive Wager

Standalone Regency
Her Counterfeit Husband (happens during A Most Unsuitable Earl)

Marriage by Deceit Series
The Earl's Secret Bargain
Love Lessons With the Duke
Ruined by the Earl
The Earl's Stolen Bride

Marriage by Arrangement Series
His Wicked Lady
Her Devilish Marquess
The Earl's Wallflower Bride

Marriage by Bargain Series
The Viscount's Runaway Bride
The Rake's Vow
Taming The Viscountess
If It Takes A Scandal

Marriage by Fate Series

The Reclusive Earl
Married In Haste
Make Believe Bride
The Perfect Duke
Kidnapping the Viscount

Marriage by Fairytale Series

The Marriage Contract
One Enchanted Evening
The Wedding Pact
Fairest of Them All
The Duke's Secluded Bride

Marriage by Necessity Series

A Perilous Marriage
The Cursed Earl – coming soon
Heiress of Misfortune – coming soon

Fairytale Regency

An Earl In Time – coming soon

Chapter One

January 1825

Miss Eris Tumilson turned thirty-five on the day she married the Duke of Jowett. She'd read the banns and purchased a new gown so she was ready on her wedding day. She gave her vows in front of family and friends. Finally, after all the years of waiting, she was a married lady.

The rest of the day was mostly spent on making sure her things were put away in her new bedchamber. At dinner, she had a pleasant conversation with her husband. He seemed as nice as her brother had assured her he'd be. She'd only talked to him a couple of times before the wedding, and her brother had been her chaperone each time. So she really didn't know much about the gentleman she'd just married. But she thought he was amiable and enjoyed his company.

She had no hesitation about marrying him, though there was some apprehension about the wedding night. As it turned out, unfortunately, her apprehension had been for nothing. She stayed up well past midnight waiting for him to come to her bedchamber, but eventually sleep overtook her. It wasn't until the sun rose that the maid told her that Jonathan had died during the course of the night.

Poor Eris had become a widow in the span of a mere twenty-four hours. All of her hopes and dreams of marriage and children were as dead as the husband she would soon have to bury.

***

Mr. Charles Duff stood by the window in the drawing room where people had gathered for the funeral of his good friend, Jonathan Taylor, the Duke of Jowett. The last time Charles had seen him had been at the wedding breakfast, and Jonathan had looked perfectly fine. He'd been laughing and talking about the future. He didn't seem sick. He'd mentioned no malady to Charles. Charles had fully expected to see him again within a day or two.

But instead of seeing his friend, Charles had received a missive telling him that his friend had died during the middle of the night. The doctor had decided the cause was a failing heart. Charles had argued with the doctor that Jonathan hadn't even been forty, but the doctor said even the young died from any number of things. "The human body is prone to mortality," the doctor had said. "No one lives forever. The only questions are how and when we'll die."

As much as Charles tried to reconcile the doctor's words, he couldn't. It just didn't seem like his friend had died of heart failure. His friend had been too full of life—too healthy—for that kind of thing.

No. Charles just couldn't bring himself to accept it. Something else was at play in this situation.

He turned his gaze to the Duchess of Jowett. She sat on the settee with her brother. Her dark hair almost matched her black gown. Her brother said something, and she offered a reply. Charles wasn't close enough to hear what they were saying. There were too many people in the room. All he could do was see her face, and it didn't seem like she was sorry her husband had died.

Charles' jaw clenched.

"Are you ready to go to the cemetery?" Charles' father, Lord Jackman, asked as he came up to him.

Charles forced his gaze off of the attractive widow and turned to his father. "I suppose there's no delaying it. Nothing's going to bring Jonathan back." He swallowed back the bitterness that threatened to rise up to the surface.

His father's expression softened. "Once we cross the threshold into the next life, there is no coming back."

No, unfortunately, there wasn't.

"We'll take Gill with us in my carriage," his father told him.

Charles looked over at his brother-in-law who was waiting near the doorway with the other gentlemen. Charles then looked at his sister who was holding her four-year-old son. She'd just found out she was expecting another child, so she wasn't showing yet. She was standing with their mother and a couple of other ladies. His family didn't know Jonathan all that well. They had come here for his sake. His other two sisters had stayed home, given their young age.

The mood was somber in the room. All funerals were this way, Charles guessed. Death was never pleasant.

At least not for everyone.

Without meaning to, Charles' gaze went back to the newly widowed Duchess of Jowett. Not a single tear. Nothing in her expression indicated that she was upset about Jonathan's death. That was telling, wasn't it? If she cared about Jonathan at all, shouldn't there be some indication on her face to convey that?

"Charles, are you coming with us to the cemetery?" his father asked.

Once more, Charles had to force his attention off of her. "Yes."

He followed his father to the carriage and sat across from the two gentlemen. Though his father and Gill talked, he let his mind wander to the past few weeks. Jonathan had been anticipating his marriage. He never said he loved Miss Tumilson, but he liked her brother and thought she was pleasant enough. The marriage had been arranged so quickly that Charles hadn't met her until the wedding day.

Could it be that Jonathan had misjudged her? Could Jonathan have been led astray by her beauty? Yes, she was older than most ladies who were looking for husbands, but she was still pleasing to the eyes. No doubt Jonathan had taken one look at her and noticed that. Charles wasn't a fool. Many gentlemen lost their wits to a pretty face, but he had believed Jonathan was wise enough to consider a lady's character, too.

It was a grim prospect to consider that a lady might do harm to her husband, but the more Charles thought about it, the more he was convinced the doctor was wrong.

The line of carriages arrived at the cemetery. Charles took in the neat rows of tombstones that the groundskeeper kept in pristine condition. Yes, this was where everyone would one day end up, but it just wasn't fair that someone so young should be taken before his time.

The carriages came to a stop. Charles waited for his father and Gill to leave before he stepped outside. He pulled the coat closer around him. The chill in the air was appropriate for a day like this. Why shouldn't death and cold go hand in hand?

He scanned the cemetery until he found the open grave where his friend's body would be laid to rest. Well, there was no delaying it. The time for the burial had come.

He had to force down the urge to cry as he watched the men lower the casket into the hole. Gentlemen didn't cry. Gentlemen had to put on a pretense of being strong at all times. They had to pretend they didn't experience things as common as sorrow or pain. Only ladies could express grief.

So why was the Duchess of Jowett not doing it? Why didn't she show the slightest trace of sorrow?

Maybe she killed Jonathan.

The thought came to him so suddenly that he stopped looking at the casket. He knew his mind had been processing everything in a way that such a conclusion was inevitable, but it still shocked him to think it. Like the others, it was difficult to accept the possibility that a lady would kill anyone, especially her husband.

But now that he'd come to the conclusion, he could accept no other line of reasoning. He knew for certain that Jonathan hadn't died from heart failure. Also, there was no one else in the townhouse except for Jonathan's bride. Well, the servants were there, but they had been there for years. There was only one person who could have harmed Jonathan in the middle of the night.

He turned his gaze back to the casket which was now securely placed in the hole. Since he was permitted to do so, he picked up a handful of fresh dirt.

"I'll never forget you, my friend," he said. *And I'm going to prove your wife killed you if it's the last thing I do.*

With the promise made, he tossed the dirt down to the casket.

***

Eris sat in front of her vanity the morning after the funeral. She didn't feel like getting dressed. She didn't feel like getting her hair styled. She didn't feel like leaving her bedchamber.

But she had to. She couldn't keep herself locked away for the rest of her life. No matter how tempting it was.

She had only been married for a day. It seemed pointless to wear black, but she supposed she had to wear that color. She glanced at the dark gowns as her lady's maid sorted through them. They all seemed to be laughing at her. *Look who is going to wear black as if she'd been with her husband for a long time.*

She should feel sorry for Jonathan. He was the one who'd been buried. But the selfish part of her, the one she tried hard to suppress, kept screaming that it wasn't fair she'd been denied the joys of having a husband. It'd only been because of her brother that Jonathan had married her. Everyone else her brother knew were already married or too young to be a suitable match for her. Jonathan had been her only chance.

At least you don't have to say you're a spinster anymore. You are a widow.

While that was true, it wasn't any real consolation. She hadn't really been a wife.

The lady's maid brought over a black gown. "Would you like to wear this one, Your Grace?"

Since the gowns were so much alike, she saw no reason to be particular. She offered a nod and let her lady's maid help her get dressed. Though there was little point in it, she allowed the lady's maid to fix her hair as if she had anywhere important to go. The truth was, she didn't have anything to look forward to.

Today, she'd sit at home and do some sewing or read a book. There was nothing to distinguish today from any other day she'd lived prior to her betrothal. She hadn't realized how much of a recluse she'd become since her mother's death. Had it not been for her brother, she wouldn't have any real interaction with the world. She had thought that marriage to Jonathan was going to change her life for the better.

She brushed the tears from her eyes before the lady's maid noticed. It was wrong for her to be selfish like this. She should feel sorry for Jonathan. He'd been a very pleasant person to be around. He didn't deserve to die. If he had lived, she had no doubt their marriage would have led to a love match.

"Is there anything else you require, Your Grace?" her lady's maid asked.

Breaking out of her thoughts, Eris turned her gaze to the mirror. Her hair was pulled back into a flattering style. It was a shame she had no one to impress.

Pushing the thought aside, she relieved the lady's maid of her duties. She remained at the vanity for a while.

It was hard to get motivated to go to the drawing room when there was nothing of interest to do. Finally, after a half hour, she forced herself to get up and left the bedchamber.

Chapter Two

"I'm glad you came," Eris said as she hugged her brother that afternoon.

"I had to see how you were doing," Mr. Byron Tumilson replied.

"There's nothing to worry about." She pulled away from him. "Jonathan's the one who isn't coming back."

"I know, but sometimes it's the ones left behind who are worse off."

She sat on the settee and waited for him to sit next to her before she said, "You know I didn't love him. I barely even knew him."

"Yes, but you would have grown to love him had he lived. He had an excellent reputation. I've heard plenty of gentlemen say that he always followed through with his word. A gentleman like that can't help but make a good husband. I wish I had gotten to know him better myself. I was hoping to do that after I successfully completed the job he hired me for."

She had to resist the urge to ask him why Jonathan had hired him. She'd never been tempted to ask him about the other cases he'd dealt with in the past, but she did wonder about this one since it had involved the gentleman she'd married.

The butler came into the room and placed the tray of tea and scones on the table in front of them.

When the butler left, she poured tea for them both and handed her brother a cup. "I don't know what to do with myself. I'm used to spending a lot of time sitting around the house, but I feel restless today."

"You expected to spend time with Jonathan. You didn't think marriage would lead to this." He gave her a sympathetic look. "I can't tell you how sorry I am."

"You didn't do anything wrong. No one could have predicted that he was going to die."

"Death, unfortunately, happens to people of all ages. I've seen it happen time and time again. Those too young go too soon. We take it for granted that we'll live to an old age."

Yes, he was right. She had assumed she and Jonathan would have many years together before either one of them died. She took a sip of the tea and watched as her brother ate the scone. After a moment, she asked, "Do you ever plan to marry?"

"I do, but I haven't met the right lady yet. I don't have a title to compel me to marry early in life. I can take my time. Though, considering everything, who knows if there's really much time for any of us?"

"Maybe I should have married anyone who would have had me while I was in my Season."

"I don't think it would have been wise to marry someone you didn't want to be with. I've heard from several gentlemen that life goes on too long if they're with wives who make them miserable. It's ideal to have a love match. I think it's better to be single forever than to be married to the wrong person."

"You're probably right. I didn't get to love Jonathan, but I think I would have."

"I know it's little consolation, but he told me he was looking forward to spending the rest of his life with you. I'm sure he thought he would grow to love you, too."

She brushed aside the tear that slid down her cheek. "Is it selfish that I feel sorry for myself?"

"No one can condemn you for feeling the way you do." He placed a comforting hand on her shoulder. "I feel sorry for you, too. This isn't what I wanted for you."

She offered him a smile to thank him for reassuring her that she wasn't a terrible person before she pulled out a handkerchief to wipe more tears away.

***

Later that day, Eris received a missive from a gentleman who referred to himself as Mr. Duff. He wrote that he was a good friend of Jonathan's and wished to speak with her. She had no idea what he could possibly want with her.

If Mr. Duff was as close to Jonathan as he claimed, he had probably been at the wedding and funeral. There had been so many people at both events. Jonathan had introduced her to all of them at the wedding breakfast, but she'd been overwhelmed by all of the people in attendance. She recalled that a lot of the same people had come to the funeral, but there were quite a few who hadn't been at the wedding.

No amount of trying to summon the image of Mr. Duff worked. She honestly had no idea who he was. Since he had been Jonathan's friend, she felt obligated to say she'd talk with him, so she wrote back and invited him to stop by the following afternoon. She had nowhere to go. She would be here when he came. She simply said he was free to come over any time he wished. Then she gave the missive to the butler and spent the rest of the day working on her embroidery.

She tried to sleep that night, but it proved to be a difficult thing to accomplish when she struggled in vain to figure out what Mr. Duff wanted with her.

She rose early the next morning and put on another black gown. On impulse, she went into Jonathan's bedchamber. This was her first time in here. Even when she had learned of his death, she hadn't dared to step into this room. It almost seemed like she was in forbidden territory. She didn't know what prompted her to go into this room now.

Boredom, perhaps. Maybe it was a desire to learn something about him she hadn't had the chance to discover in the brief time they'd had together. Or, even more likely, it could be the desire to seek out clues as to why Mr. Duff wished to pay her a visit.

The visit might have nothing to do with her. It could have everything to do with Jonathan. Jonathan might have something that belonged to Mr. Duff. Maybe Mr. Duff wanted it back. Or maybe there was some keepsake Mr. Duff wished to have. If her friend had died, it might offer her comfort to have something special to remember her friend by.

She took her time in looking around the room. It was light and cheery, much like Jonathan had been whenever she'd seen him. The curtains were pulled back, allowing plenty of sunlight into the space, and he had chosen bright blue colors for his bedding.

On the dresser were his fob watch, a ring with a large ruby in it, gloves, and a hat. She recognized those items. She didn't, however, recognize the silver cup on the other side of the dresser. She picked it up. It didn't have anything etched into it. She had no idea what the significance could be, but maybe Mr. Duff would inquire about it. It could very well be a keepsake of some kind. After setting it back down, she noted the cane propped up against the dresser. She recalled the cane. He had used it when they went for a walk with her brother. She remembered thinking it went well with his outfit.

She opened the armoire and saw his clothes. It was a shame he'd never wear any of these again. She supposed there was no point in keeping them. It wasn't like she could wear them. She closed the doors and went to the small room off to the side of his bedchamber. There wasn't much in it. Just a desk and a chair. Parchment and an inkwell rested on top of the desk.

She left the room and gave one more look around his bedchamber, doing her best to memorize the items in case Mr. Duff requested something from here. Satisfied, she went downstairs.

The rest of the morning passed without incident. The butler did give her a reply from Mr. Duff saying he'd be by to see her at two, but other than that, she silently worked on her embroidery.

At ten minutes to two, she asked the butler to bring in black tea and crumpets. Jonathan liked those, and she figured since Mr. Duff had been his friend, he might enjoy them as well. After the butler went to do as she wished, she stood by the window and watched for Mr. Duff's arrival. The minutes on the clock passed abnormally slow, and even the butler had returned with the tea and crumpets before a carriage came to a stop in front of her townhouse.

A gentleman in black clothes stepped out of it. His hat obscured her view of his face until he looked up at the front door. Yes, she remembered him now. He'd been the only gentleman in the room during the funeral who'd been standing at the window. Everyone else had been talking to someone. But she couldn't recall if he'd been at the wedding. No one had been standing apart from the crowd on her wedding day.

His gaze went to the windows, and she instinctively stepped back. She was sure he hadn't seen her, but her pulse still raced at the thought of being caught watching him.

She hurried to the small table near the chairs and poured tea into the cups, doing her best not to notice the way her hands shook. She was no good at entertaining guests she didn't know. One would think the older she got, the easier it would be to talk to others. The opposite, however, seemed to be the case.

She heard footsteps approach and forced her grip to remain steady as she set the teapot down. She straightened up and wiped her hands on her gown. There was nothing to be nervous about. He probably just wanted to ask if he could have something that once belonged to Jonathan. If so, she thought the silver cup might make a nice keepsake.

The footman came into the room, and her gaze went to the dark-haired gentleman with brown eyes. He stood taller than most, and he had broad shoulders and a lean build.

"Mr. Duff, Your Grace," the footman introduced.

Mr. Duff bowed, so she gave a slight curtsy to return the greeting. Then she cleared her throat and gestured to the chair closest to the table. "Won't you have a seat, Mr. Duff?"

Mr. Duff offered a nod, and she gestured to the footman that he could go. She went to a nearby chair and held the cup out to Mr. Duff, doing her best to keep her grip steady.

Fortunately, she was successful. She hated it when she gave visible signs of her apprehension. She retrieved her cup and settled back into her chair. She hurried to take a few sips of her tea so she could avoid having to be the first person who spoke.

"Thank you for agreeing to see me," Mr. Duff said. "I'm sure you have many things to do. I'll be mindful of your time."

"You were Jonathan's friend," she replied. "I will take as much time as you want." Never mind that she had nothing to do.

"Yes, I was his friend." His voice grew soft, and his gaze went to the cup in his hand. He put the cup down and took a deep breath. "I was his friend since we were fifteen."

Maybe he was as nervous as she was. Hoping to put him at ease, she said, "I don't mind it if you want something that belonged to him."

His eyebrows furrowed. "You don't?"

"I figured since you were his friend, you came here to get a keepsake. When my father and mother passed on to the next life, I took comfort in taking something that belonged to each of them." She shrugged. "I know it's not the same as having the person still with you, but it's a nice reminder that they used to be alive. It's something tangible you can hold onto."

"It would be nice to have something that belonged to him." He paused. "I would like to have his cane, if it's still here."

"You can have it. I'll be happy to get it for you."

She got ready to stand up, but he stopped her. "There's no rush. I thought we'd talk for a while."

"Oh, all right." She settled back into the chair. "What did you wish to talk about?"

"Jonathan didn't say much about you. I figured that was because the marriage had been arranged so suddenly." He smiled. "There had to be something special about you to make him pick you instead of someone else."

"I don't know if it was me so much as my brother." She shifted in the chair. "My brother met him a few months ago, and the two seemed to strike up a friendship. They had no trouble talking to each other. Do you know my brother? He's Mr. Tumilson."

"The name sounds familiar, but I'm having trouble putting it with a face."

Recalling that Mr. Duff had been at the funeral by the window, she said, "I was sitting with him on the settee before you and the others left for Jonathan's burial. Does that help you remember what he looks like?"

"You know I was at the funeral?"

"I recognize you. You were standing by the window."

"Do you remember me from the wedding?"

Her face grew warm. "Unfortunately, no. I only remember you from the funeral because you were standing by yourself. Everyone else was talking to someone."

"I was at the wedding," he said. "Jonathan introduced us."

She offered him an apologetic smile. "He introduced me to a lot of people that day. Unless there's something to separate someone from the crowd, I have trouble remembering people, and there are a lot of gentlemen with dark hair in London."

"Forgive me. I didn't mean to sound as if I'm accusing you of doing something wrong." He took a sip of tea then added, "To answer your question, I don't know your brother beyond that of a very casual acquaintance. I met him before the wedding. He was here once when I came by to visit my friend. That's when I met him. I don't suppose your brother mentioned me at all?"

"No. Jonathan was probably discussing something of a private nature when you saw them. My brother never tells me who he meets while he's on the job."

"Really? What does your brother do?"

"He's a Runner."

His eyebrows furrowed. "He investigates things for people?"

She nodded. "It's not steady employment, but if someone suspects there's a crime, they hire him to investigate matters."

"Jonathan never mentioned something wrong to me. What kind of things does your brother investigate?"

"Well, it can be anything, really. It can be as simple as someone who misplaces something that needs to be tracked down. Or it can be something as complicated as figuring out who's been stealing money. He's worked for gentlemen of nobility and those of the middle class."

"I wonder why Jonathan didn't tell me why he was talking to your brother. You said your brother's name is Mr. Tumilson, correct?"

"Yes, it is. I'm not sure how many people know about him. Runners have a better reputation than they used to, but I suspect he doesn't advertise what he does because some people still don't trust them to be honest. My brother never takes a bribe. In fact, the other Runners he knows are doing everything they can to keep their reputations in good standing."

"I'm not familiar with Runners, but I applaud him for his efforts to keep his reputation untouched by scandal."

She waited to see if he would continue, but he fell into silence. Since she didn't know what to say, she decided to pick up a crumpet and eat it. He wasn't asking if she would get the cane. He might still want to talk to her. Or, maybe he was done talking but didn't want to seem rude by asking for the cane. He could be waiting for her to offer to get it for him.

She swallowed the last of her crumpet then asked, "Would you like me to bring down Jonathan's cane now?"

"If you don't mind, I'd appreciate having it."

Glad she had thought to ask, she rose to her feet. "I won't be long."

"You're not going to summon the butler to get it?" he asked, not hiding his surprise.

"I was in Jonathan's bedchamber earlier today. I know where it is. You don't mind being here alone for a little while, do you?"

"No, I don't mind."

With a promise to be quick, she hurried out of the room.

Chapter Three

Charles watched as Jonathan's widow slipped out of the room. He relaxed and settled back in the chair. It was difficult to maintain a pleasant disposition around someone who had something to hide.

She killed Jonathan. There was no doubt about it. She had trouble meeting his gaze. She kept shifting in the chair. Her hands trembled while she was drinking and eating. There was even a slight waver in her voice. All signs pointed to her being guilty.

The problem was that he had to prove it. Obviously, he couldn't come right out and accuse her. She'd only deny it.

No, he had to be smart about this. He couldn't let her know he knew the truth. He was going to have to be better than her. She was clever. She'd managed to fool everyone. Even the doctor didn't believe there was anything suspicious about Jonathan's untimely death. And if she was telling him the truth, that her brother was a

Runner, then he bet she had picked up little tricks from him on getting away with crimes.

He had to figure this out, and he had to do it without arousing her suspicions. He was going to have to get close to her if he was going to prove she murdered his friend. And to do that, he was going to have to seem genuinely interested in her.

When she returned to the drawing room with the cane, he stood up to take it from her. "Thank you."

He turned the cane over in his hands. Yes, it was Jonathan's. He recognized the nick in the handle. Jonathan had dropped it by accident when they were walking down the steps of Lord Clement's ball. That had been a year ago. He forced back the lump in his throat.

"I wish I had gotten to know him better," she said, her voice soft. "He seemed like such a wonderful person."

"He was," Charles replied. It took all of his willpower not to demand she tell him why she killed him. Instead, he forced himself to meet her gaze and added, "Some people are gone much too soon."

She nodded and lowered her gaze.

An admission of guilt. He was sure of it. He glanced over at the rest of the tea and crumpets. He couldn't find a reason to linger here, and it was likely that she'd grow suspicious if he didn't leave now that he'd gotten the cane.

He gave her a smile that hinted at flirtation and said, "I look forward to seeing you again."

She seemed as if she didn't know how to respond, and since it gave him the advantage, he wished her a pleasant afternoon then left the townhouse. He wasn't sure he could keep coming to this townhouse to visit her. What he needed was to have some chance encounter with her. Otherwise, it would be too obvious. He had to be careful. He had to outwit her.

He got into his carriage and gripped the cane. It was ridiculous how many people thought she had planned to make a life with his friend. All she'd wanted was his money. It was no secret that Jonathan made a lot of money in the past year. He had become one of the most attractive bachelors in a very short time. She had come along and claimed him. She probably used her brother to accomplish her goal.

If only Jonathan had told him more about her.

If only he had thought to ask Jonathan more details about her and why he had agreed to the marriage.

He set his head against the back of the seat and closed his eyes. There was no point in going over the things he should have done. It wasn't going to solve anything. All he could do was avenge his friend's death, and the only way to do that was to prove his bride had murdered him. And he was going to do just that. One way or another, he was going to see to it that justice prevailed.

***

"Won't you join the rest of us and play cards?" Heather Easton, Viscountess Powell, asked as she approached the chair.

Charles looked up from the cane he was holding. His sister stood in front of him, a concerned expression on her face.

"I shouldn't have come tonight," Charles said. "It's not right that I should enjoy myself while Jonathan lies in the grave. I should be alone in my room like our younger sisters are."

"It's just a game of cards," she replied. "You're not going to a ball or the theatre. You've been in your home for the past two weeks since the funeral. Father and Mother are right. You need to be a part of life. Jonathan would want that."

"I know. He was the kindest person who ever lived."

He forced back his tears. It was difficult to go through so many emotions. At times, he was so determined to avenge his friend's death that he was too angry to cry. Then at other times, like now, all he could do was dwell on the fact that he'd never see Jonathan again. All he had was the cane, and the cane was a lousy substitute for his friend.

With a sigh, Heather knelt in front of him. "He was kind. Kinder than most. It's not fair that he's gone. Perhaps Gill and I shouldn't have had a dinner party this evening. We only wished to cheer you up."

He glanced over at the table where their parents, their nineteen-year-old cousin, and Gill were playing cards. They were all here to cheer him up. It wasn't their fault their plan hadn't worked. They had promised a quiet dinner and a relaxing evening. It was a promise they had kept. He just couldn't bring himself to go along with it.

All he could think about was the last time he'd seen Jonathan. That had been at the wedding breakfast. Jonathan had seemed so happy. He was looking forward to the rest of his life. Little did any of them know he'd never live to see another sunrise.

"I'm sorry," Charles said. "I shouldn't have come. I'm just not in the mood for this."

He stood up, and she rose to her feet.

He stepped around her and went to the table where the others were playing cards. Charles stopped as an idea came to him.

His cousin might be nineteen, but she was a lady. Ladies had liberties gentlemen didn't. They could visit other ladies and take walks with each other whenever they wanted. He'd been struggling to come up with a way to see Jonathan's widowed bride again. His cousin very well could be the answer he was looking for.

"Reina, may I have a moment with you in private?" Charles asked his cousin.

Reina wiped a blonde wisp of hair from her eyes then put her cards down. "All right. I was going to lose this hand anyway."

Ignoring the curious stares from the others, Charles led her over to the corner and waited until the others resumed their card game before softly asking, "How good are you at keeping secrets?"

"Did you hear about the thing that happened to my mother two years ago?" she asked.

"Something happened to your mother?"

"You don't know because I didn't tell you."

"Tell me what?"

"I'm not telling you."

Realizing she'd been making a point, he smiled. "That's good."

She returned his smile. "I might be young, but I have my wits about me."

"Can you also pretend to be friends with someone?"

Not hiding her surprise, she said, "I suppose, but I've never had a need to do that. What is this about?"

"I can't go into detail, but I need to get better acquainted with a lady and I don't know how to do it without seeming too obvious."

Her eyes lit up. "I had no idea you fancied someone."

He debated whether he should tell her that he was only pretending he was interested in the widow, but it might be best if she thought he was sincerely interested in her.

"Do you want your sister to help, too?" Reina asked.

"No. Heather's expecting a child, and she has her own family to think about."

"Oh, that's understandable."

"There's no need to tell her. Or the others. I'd rather keep this just between us."

"You have no need to worry. I won't say a word to anyone." She let out a quiet cheer and patted him on the arm. "I can't wait to do my part for true love. When should I start my role?"

Since she was so willing to do it, he ventured, "Is tomorrow too soon?"

"Tomorrow's perfect. I have nothing to do. Where should I meet her?"

"At her townhouse."

She bit her lower lip then asked, "You want me to go to her townhouse without her permission?"

"Not exactly." He glanced at the others who were finishing up their game. "We'll talk about it tomorrow. I don't want to risk them hearing."

"All right. I can't wait to find out what we're going to do."

He watched her as she returned to the card table. He probably should play at least one hand, but the truth was, he would only lose. He had much to plan. He needed to come up with an excuse to get Reina to meet Jonathan's widow. Everything had to be done just right. He couldn't leave out a single detail.

Grasping the cane more firmly in his hand, he went to his family, excused himself for the evening, and took his carriage home.

Chapter Four

Eris was reading a book when the footman told her someone by the name of Miss Reina Livingstone had gotten lost and needed help finding her destination. Eris told him to bring her into the room before she marked her place in the book and set it aside.

A moment later, a lady who appeared to be at least ten years younger than her came into the drawing room. Though she wore a thick coat, her cheeks were warm from being out in the chilly weather.

"Would you like something hot to drink?" Eris offered.

"I don't wish to trouble you," the lady said. "I was on my way to the market. I'm not sure how it happened, but I ended up in an entire section of townhouses. I should have taken a carriage. The day was so nice I decided to go for a walk, but, as you can tell, that wasn't a good decision."

Eris smiled. "London is a big place. It's easy for anyone to get lost, especially when the townhouses are so similar."

"Yes, they are similar. It's hard to tell one street from another."

"What part of the market were you going to?"

"I need new boots, so I was going to Johnson & Sons Shoe Company. I heard they have the best quality."

"They do. I've been using them for years."

Reina's eyes lit up. "Would you be willing to show me where that shop is? I've only been in London for a couple of weeks. I haven't done much shopping."

"I'll be more than happy to take you there," Eris said, secretly glad to have something to do. While the book she'd been reading was entertaining, she was tired of being by herself all day.

"Thank you. I can't tell you how relieved I am to have someone show me where it is. I had directions, but, as you see, I got lost."

Eris smiled. "Before we go, you should have some hot tea. It'll warm you up, and it'll give the coachman time to get the carriage ready."

Before Eris could make it to the cord on the wall, Reina called out, "Can't we walk there?"

Eris paused and turned to face her. "We could, but it looks like you've done a lot of walking already." She gestured to Reina's pink cheeks.

Reina touched them then shrugged. "I don't feel cold. I feel fine. It's rather pleasant outside."

Eris supposed a walk wouldn't do either of them any harm. Besides, walking meant she'd spend more time out of this townhouse, and that would make the day pass faster. She had all the time she wanted to sit and read when she came back.

"All right," Eris agreed. "We'll walk, but I'll still have the butler bring us something to drink." She reached the cord and pulled on it. "What kind of tea do you like?"

"Oh, um, I suppose black tea."

Eris returned to her visitor and encouraged Reina to take off her coat and hat. "You might as well be comfortable while we have tea," Eris said.

Reina removed them. "This is awfully kind of you."

"I have plenty of tea and time. It's no trouble." Eris took the items from her and placed them on a nearby chair just as the butler came into the room. After she asked him to bring tea up, she returned to her visitor. "I won't keep you any more than fifteen minutes."

She gestured to the chairs closest to the fire, and the two sat down.

"I hope my question won't make you uncomfortable," Eris began, "but don't you have a guardian who can show you around London?"

"I do. I live with my aunt and uncle, and they usually take me where I need to go. Today I thought it'd be nice to take a walk by myself. I thought I knew my way around enough to find the market, but apparently, I don't. In the future, I'll just take a carriage when I'm alone. Then this won't happen again."

Noting the contrite expression on Reina's face, she said, "There's no point in being hard on yourself. It's an easy mistake anyone can make. I'm sure after this, you'll know exactly where the market is."

"I hope you're right." She paused then asked, "How long have you lived here?"

"I've been here my entire life."

Reina's eyes widened. "You have? I thought everyone in the noble classes had a home in the country."

"Oh, well, I wasn't born a duchess. I married a duke. My family comes from the middle class. We manage fine, but we don't have the kind of money nobility does."

"Not all of the nobility has a lot of money. It just seems that way. Everyone wants to give the impression of wealth. A lot of marriages are made for financial reasons."

Really? Eris had no idea such was the case. She'd always gotten the impression they had more money than they could spend in a lifetime.

"It's preferable to marry for love," Reina said as the butler came back into the room. "I want to marry for love."

"I think everyone wants to marry for love," Eris replied.

The two waited until the butler left them alone with the tea before continuing their conversation.

"Did you love the duke?" Reina asked.

Eris sipped her tea. "I barely knew him. It was a marriage my brother arranged for me. From the little I knew of him, I liked him. I think we could have had a love match if he'd lived long enough."

Reina gave her a sympathetic look. "I'm sorry he wasn't able to live that long." She drank some tea then added, "But you shouldn't give up. You might find someone you'll fall in love with."

"I'm in my mid-thirties. I've passed my ideal time for marriage. The Duke of Jowett was my only chance."

"You mustn't say that. It's very possible there might be someone else. You're not an old lady."

"I'm not young, either."

"There are plenty of gentlemen who don't marry in their twenties."

"That's different. They can have children at any age. A lady's ability to have children is limited."

"But there's more to marriage than children. There's companionship. It'd be nice to have someone who understands you better than anyone else, wouldn't it? This would be someone you can feel safe with, who accepts you just as you are without passing any judgments."

"Yes, but you can get that kind of companionship without a husband. My brother and I can talk to each other about anything, and we support each other no matter what happens."

"The kind of companionship you can have with a husband would go deeper than that. Imagine being able to have the same closeness you do with your brother but have the gentleman hold and kiss you, too."

Eris knew what Reina was getting at, and she had to agree it would be nice. That was what she'd been missing in her life. It was why she jumped at the chance to marry Jonathan. She was looking forward to the possibility of falling in love with him. It was a shame that possibility had been taken from her.

No, it's not fair for you to be selfish. Jonathan's the one you should feel sorry for. He's dead, and he has no heir.

There wasn't even the chance he had an heir. They hadn't even consummated the marriage. She had to resist the urge to feel sorry for herself again. In addition to being a widow, she would also be childless. She shook the thought off. Poor Jonathan was in the cemetery, and all she could do was feel sorry for herself.

"You're an attractive lady," Reina told her. "I'm sure there's a gentleman out there who wants to be with you."

Since Reina was trying so hard to be nice, Eris decided not to keep arguing with her. Reina was a lively person. She had a certain sweetness and innocence about her that Eris suspected most gentlemen liked. Unlike her, Reina shouldn't have any trouble finding a husband.

Reina glanced at the clock above the fireplace mantle. Eris looked at the time and realized she had kept her twenty minutes instead of the fifteen she promised her. She hurried to finish her tea then rose to her feet.

"I'll go upstairs to get into something warm, and then I'll take you to the market," Eris promised before she hurried out of the room.

***

Charles took another look at his pocket watch and spun on his heel to pace back down the street that was full of businesses. Where was Reina? He had taken her to the street the Duchess of Jowett lived on and showed her which townhouse she needed to go to.

Was it possible she hadn't gone to the right one? Did she get lost on her way there? He thought he'd been specific about the one she needed. He'd even been careful to describe the knocker Jonathan had put on the front door. Surely, she had noticed it.

Maybe he should have had the coachman pull the carriage directly to the townhouse. Jonathan's widow might have seen them, but at least he would know Reina was all right.

Just as Charles was about to go to his coachman and tell him to go to Jonathan's townhouse, he saw Reina and Jonathan's widow coming down the street. Relieved, he put his hand over his heart. Thank goodness. He was beginning to believe he had unwittingly put Reina in harm's way. He didn't think anyone would abduct an unescorted lady in the daytime, but the thought had suddenly worried him.

He slipped the pocket watch into his pocket and moved into the doorway of one of the shops. When they were two shops away from him, he pretended to leave the shop. He purposely looked away from them before he turned his gaze in their direction. He feigned surprise and called out a greeting to Reina.

She waved a greeting in return and led Jonathan's widow over to him.

"I didn't expect to see you here," he told Reina.

"I need a new pair of boots," Reina replied, using the line they had rehearsed. "The Duchess of Jowett was kind enough to show me where the market was. I forgot how to get here. London is much bigger than I realized." She turned to the duchess and added, "This is my cousin, Mr. Duff."

"We met," Her Grace said.

"Yes," Charles added. "She was kind enough to give me my friend's cane so I could have something to remember him by. She was the one who married my good friend who recently passed on to the next life."

On cue, Reina's eyes grew wide and she asked, "Oh, was he the Duke of Jowett? I didn't realize." She put her hand to her cheek and turned back to the duchess. "You'll have to forgive me. I only arrived to London two weeks ago. That was after the funeral."

"It's just as well you weren't here for it," Charles said. "There's nothing more tragic than watching someone you care about be taken to the cemetery." He glanced at the duchess to see how she'd respond to that comment, but she didn't seem to be affected by it. While he knew Jonathan hadn't known her all that well, she could at least pretend to be upset at his passing. Forcing his attention back to Reina, he smiled. "I don't want to ruin a pleasant day with sorrow. My friend was a happy person. He brought joy wherever he went." He cleared his throat. "Are you both shopping?"

"I don't know." Reina's gaze went to the duchess. "Do you need anything while we're here?"

"No, I have everything I need," the duchess said.

"Since you two walked all the way here, I'd be remiss if I didn't offer you a ride back home in my carriage. It's right there." He gestured further down the street where his coachman waited at the carriage.

"Thank you for the offer," Reina said. "I hated the thought of Her Grace having to walk all the way back to her townhouse."

"Walking doesn't bother me," Jonathan's widow replied. "It's nice to get outside and do something."

"While I appreciate you being gracious, I still wish I hadn't interrupted what you were doing just so you could take me down here," Reina said.

"You didn't interrupt anything I can't do later." The duchess' gaze swept across the shops. "Johnson & Sons Shoe Company is right there."

Reina glanced at the building. "So it is. Would you like to come with me? Then we can take you home, unless there's somewhere else my cousin needs to go first?"

"No, I have nowhere else to shop." He patted his pocket. "I already found a new chain for my pocket watch."

"If it won't bore you, you might as well join us," Reina said.

He nodded and went with them to the boot shop. Reina was doing a marvelous job. If he didn't know better, he would think she sincerely enjoyed being with Jonathan's widow.

As Reina tried on a pair of boots, Charles glanced over at the duchess, who was sitting next to him. "Thank you for bringing my cousin here. I was getting worried about her. I thought she knew her way around London better than this."

She offered him a smile. "I was happy to bring her to the market. I was going to bring her in my carriage, but she insisted on walking."

Reina had done that in order to give him an excuse to take her back to her townhouse. It would offer him a few extra minutes with her, and those extra few minutes might give him an advantage. Any opportunity, no matter how small, could lead to a clue.

"I hope you don't mind that I insisted she have some tea," the lady next to him continued. "That's what took us so long to get here. I didn't realize you were waiting for her."

"It's fine that you had tea with her. I don't mind." He hadn't thought that she was going to give Reina some tea since Reina was only supposed to tell her she needed to get to the shops, but it did provide him with a way to get her to see Reina—and him—again. "As you know, my cousin is new here. I think it'd be nice if she made some friends. My sister is a lovely person, but she has a husband

and a child who take up a lot of her time. My cousin could use the companionship of another lady."

"I like your cousin. She seems like a sweet person."

"She is. And if you don't mind me saying so, it seems like you two already get along well. Now that she knows where you live, would you mind it if she came by to pay you a visit?"

"I wouldn't mind."

So far, this conversation was going exactly as he hoped. All he had to do was add the final part. He cleared his throat. "If I happen to be chaperoning her for the day, do you mind if I bring her in my carriage?"

"Of course not. Both of you are welcome to visit."

Good. That was all he needed. It would be easy to come up with reasons to come with Reina. Now he just needed to come up with subtle ways to express an interest in the duchess. He couldn't do that in public. He'd need a private setting, and the drawing room of her townhouse would suffice.

Reina glanced his way after she was done testing out a pair of boots. He gave her a slight nod to let her know he had accomplished what he wanted.

She turned to the store owner and told him, "I'll take these."

"Are you sure there are no shops you want to go to while we're at the market?" Charles asked the duchess.

"No, I'm fine," the duchess replied. "I meant what I said before. I have everything I need."

Charles just bet she did. Jonathan had more than enough money to see to it that his widow would be well provided for. Charles recalled how many years Jonathan had carefully invested and saved. Jonathan had wanted to make sure he was ready for a wife and children when he married. Little did he know that as soon as he got the wife, all of that wealth would go to her immediately.

Charles supposed there might be a child. Jonathan did live to see a part of his wedding night. Charles bet she made sure to consummate the marriage before she murdered him. After all, a widow with a child was the very image of innocence. No one would ever think her capable of murder if they found out she was expecting Jonathan's child.

Who was Charles kidding? No one suspected her of murder now. It was up to him to prove it. That's why he was doing this. His friend couldn't rest in his grave until people knew the truth.

Reina gestured to Charles that the owner was ready for the money. Charles rose to his feet and paid him. Afterward, he escorted both ladies to the carriage.

On the way to Jonathan's townhouse, Charles watched as Reina and the duchess talked. They really did seem to get along well. One would swear they had known each other forever with the way they were talking.

When the carriage stopped in front of Jonathan's townhouse, the duchess thanked them. Charles took the opportunity to give her a smile he hoped would suggest a shy romantic interest in her. If she noticed, he didn't know. He watched her as she walked up the steps to his friend's townhouse. It was hard to believe that only a month ago, he'd gone there to spend an afternoon playing cards and discussing books with him.

"I like her," Reina said as the carriage moved forward. "I can see why you fancy her. She's pretty and kind."

"I asked her if she'd mind if I happened to come along with you when you paid her a visit, but I aimed to be subtle about my intentions," Charles replied. "I don't want to be obvious."

"You weren't obvious at all. She might suspect you have an interest in her, but she doesn't know for certain."

"That's what I was hoping," he lied. After a moment, he added, "Next time we come here, it should be on a rainy day. That way you won't be out taking a walk, and I can bring you while I'm on my way to meet a friend." He shrugged. "Or something."

"That's perfect! I think I'll whisper in her ear something about you that will spark her interest. And you needn't worry. I'll do it when you aren't looking so she won't know we're planning this whole thing together. I don't think she knows why we're really talking to her."

"No, I don't, either. You're good at acting."

"Well, considering how nice she is, I wouldn't really call it acting. But yes, we do have another reason for all of this." She winked and giggled. "It's so much fun to be a matchmaker."

"Just remember to keep it all a secret. No one else in the family must find out."

"I won't tell a soul. This will only be between you and me."

Good because if the rest of his family found out, they'd never understand. They would assume he was jumping to conclusions. They would only say he was falsely accusing the poor widow. As long as they were unaware of what was happening, he shouldn't have any problems.

Chapter Five

Two days later, Eris received a missive from Reina asking if she could visit her. Excited, Eris sent a response back and made sure to have black tea and scones ready by the time Reina arrived. But Reina wasn't alone. She came with her cousin.

"I hope you don't mind that he's with me," Reina said as Eris led them to the chairs in the drawing room that were by the fireplace. "With it raining out, I didn't want to walk. He brought me in his carriage."

"I don't mind," Eris replied. "I'll have the butler bring another cup." Once she instructed the butler to do so, she returned to her visitors and sat down. "How do the boots feel?" she asked Reina.

"They're very comfortable," Reina replied.

"I'm glad to hear it." Eris poured tea into two cups and offered them to Reina and Mr. Duff. "The wrong kind of boots can hurt your feet."

"Well, I feel like I could walk forever in these." Reina wiggled her feet, showing off the new boots. "They are the best pair I ever had. Maybe we should go for a walk in the park."

"Not today," Mr. Duff inserted. "You need to wait for a day when it's not raining." He glanced at Eris. "Would such an outing be all right?"

Eris wasn't sure if he meant to join them on this walk or not. Was there something in his expression that indicated he wanted to go because of her? After a moment, she decided that couldn't be the case. He was only asking on behalf of Reina.

Eris cleared her throat and directed her attention to Reina. "I would love to go for a walk when it's nicer out. Have you been to Hyde Park yet?"

"No, not yet, but I've heard so much about it," Reina replied. "It sounds like the most notable people in the Ton take walks and even ride horses there."

The butler returned with the cup, and Eris took it as Mr. Duff said, "My dear cousin is fascinated with all of the people in London."

"I came all the way from the country where nothing ever happens," Reina added. "It's so exciting to hear all the stories of what people are doing."

Mr. Duff shot Reina a pointed look as the butler left. "I hope you aren't reading the *Tittletattle*. I told you that it's nothing but a haven for gossip."

Reina shook her head. "No, I don't read it. If something is real, I want to know about it, but I see no point in wasting time on things that are made up."

Based on the things Byron had told her, Eris thought there was a lot more truth in those scandal sheets than Mr. Duff realized, but she agreed it probably wasn't best for a young lady to waste her time reading such things. She poured tea into her cup and picked up a scone.

"It sounds like Lord and Lady Cadwalader are the most influential people in London," Reina said after silence fell among the group.

"I'd say that's an accurate statement," Mr. Duff replied before he took a drink of his tea. "If you want to have a good Season, my suggestion is not to do anything to upset them."

Reina's eyes grew wide. "Why? Are they vengeful?"

"I don't know if I'd say they're vengeful," he slowly replied as if choosing his words with great care. "But they do impact who will or who won't talk to you. As long as you're careful to abide by the rules, you'll be fine. We'll find a nice, honorable gentleman for you to marry soon enough."

"I am looking forward to meeting available gentlemen." Reina's gaze went to Eris. "I haven't been able to meet anyone who's looking for a wife yet. I'm still learning the proper etiquette and how to do the steps to the dances."

"There is a lot to learn," Eris said. "I don't envy you having to go through all of that."

"But you learned it at one time," Reina replied.

"Yes," Eris agreed, "but I also grew up here, so I knew everything by the time I was ready for my Season."

Though, looking back on everything, she didn't see how any of those things made any difference. She might not have suffered the scorn of the Cadwaladers, but she hadn't attracted the attention of any gentlemen, either. She'd heard of ladies who had upset the Cadwaladers who went on to marry gentlemen and have children. Because of that, she didn't see how damaging a scandal was to a lady's future. She could, however, understand why Mr. Duff didn't want his cousin to suffer the Ton's disapproval, so she wasn't about to encourage the lady to dismiss the rules.

Reina swallowed her scone then said, "I wouldn't mind some advice on how to get a suitor."

At first, Eris thought she was talking to Mr. Duff, but when Mr. Duff and Reina looked expectantly at her, she realized Reina actually expected her to address this concern. She didn't know how to respond. If she knew how to get a suitor, she would have done it long ago.

After an uncomfortable moment, she finally said, "My marriage was arranged for me, and it happened long after I had my Seasons."

"My friend was looking forward to your marriage," Mr. Duff spoke up. "You must have said or done something to attract him."

She wished she knew what that something was. "I think my brother flattered me when he arranged the marriage."

"You shouldn't be so modest," Reina said. "I can't imagine how a brother can convince anyone to marry someone. Even if my dear cousin were to talk about me as if I was the most beautiful and sweetest lady in all of London, the gentleman would have to meet me in order to agree to a marriage."

"Not all marriages are made before the gentleman and lady meet," Eris replied.

"But yours was, wasn't it?" Reina asked.

"Well, yes," Eris said.

Reina sipped her tea. "Then you had to have said and done something to make him agree to the arrangement."

Eris shifted in the chair. She knew they meant to be complimentary, but they were only making her uncomfortable.

"If I might be so bold," Mr. Duff began, "I think I can answer the question. She has an innocent way about her that draws you in. It's something gentlemen find charming. She's every bit a lady. Gentlemen like to marry someone who will be a good wife and mother. Also, it helps that she's nice to look at."

Eris tried to ignore the flutter in her stomach, but Reina glanced her way and gave her a look that suggested her cousin was attracted to her. But he couldn't be. Mr. Duff was merely being polite. He wasn't here because he found her to his liking. He was only here because Reina had wanted to come by and pay her a visit.

Wasn't he?

Mr. Duff turned his gaze back to Eris. "I think it'd be marvelous if Reina could get some advice from you about making herself desirable to gentlemen. But, you don't have to do it if you don't want to. The last thing we want to do is make you uncomfortable."

Something in his eyes compelled her to say yes. Sure she had to be blushing, she said, "I'll do whatever I can to help Reina."

"Thank you!" Reina exclaimed. "I won't be so nervous now. There's a lot of pressure for a lady to find a husband in London."

Reina was telling her!

They went on to discuss the things that Reina could do once spring and summer came. Eris found herself enjoying the conversation so much that twenty minutes passed in the blink of an eye. She wished it could have lasted longer, but Reina and Mr. Duff said they had to leave.

"I had a wonderful time," Reina told her as they stood up.

"I did, too," Eris replied.

"Next time, we should go for a walk." Reina gestured to her boots. "I want to try them out and see if it's like walking on the clouds like the shop owner claimed."

Eris chuckled. "I think he was exaggerating just a little in order to secure the sale, but I also think your feet will feel better than they did in your other boots."

"I can't wait to find out!" Reina gave her a quick hug then headed out of the drawing room.

Eris blinked in surprise that Reina should leave the room before Mr. Duff had a chance to escort her out.

Before she could give it much thought, Mr. Duff took her hand and kissed it. "I can't thank you enough for your kindness toward my cousin." Then he gave her a smile that made her weak in the knees and followed after Reina.

It took Eris a moment before she could move. And when she did, all she could think of was how nice and warm his lips were.

***

"My cousin likes you," Reina said three days later as she and Eris walked in Hyde Park. "He couldn't stop talking about you after we left your townhouse. He even called you charming and beautiful."

Though Eris experienced a tingle of pleasure from Reina's words, she was sure Mr. Duff just couldn't be interested in her in the way Reina assumed. Gentlemen didn't take an interest in her. Not unless her brother was there to arrange the marriage. She still didn't understand what had made Jonathan agree to it. She was older than most ladies when they married. Younger ladies had more time to give their husbands a child. So while she was sure the promise of an heir had something to do with it, there had to be something else that had prompted Jonathan to pick her.

"What do you think of him?" Reina asked, breaking her out of her thoughts.

Thinking of Mr. Duff, Eris rubbed the hand he had kissed. Thankfully, both hands were in a muff so Reina didn't notice. "Your cousin is very nice."

"That's not what I meant." Reina's eyes sparkled. "I meant what do you think of him as a suitor? He'd make a good one. I can tell that by how attentive he is. Whenever you speak, he pays close attention, and he looks at you in a way that I hope a gentleman will look at me someday."

"You must be seeing things that aren't really happening." Eris didn't know if she was saying that to Reina or herself. The last thing she wanted was to get her hopes up. She'd had enough of that when she was in her Seasons.

"I'm not seeing anything that isn't there. He might be too shy to come out and say it, but the attraction is undeniable."

Again, Eris rubbed the back of her hand. "It's too soon. My husband hasn't been dead for more than a month."

"If you had fallen in love with him, I'd say you're right, but you told me you barely knew him."

"I owe it to his memory to refrain from having a suitor." Even as Eris said it, she couldn't believe the words that were coming from her mouth. She and Reina were both taking it for granted that Mr. Duff was interested in her. They could be wrong. They could be seeing things that weren't there.

"Why do you have to refrain from having a suitor when your husband is dead?"

"Because it's not appropriate for me to entertain the affections of another gentleman until the proper time of mourning has passed."

"And how long is that?"

"A year."

"An entire year?"

"Well, it was my husband who died," Eris said.

"But you didn't even know him that well, and you were only married for a day. How can anyone expect you to wait a year?"

Eris shrugged. "It's London. There are rules to follow."

"That rule seems ridiculous if you ask me. Imagine telling a lady that she can't let a gentleman who's obviously interested in her to be her suitor because of some silly rule. If you had been married for years, that would make sense." She paused then asked, "Do all ladies follow this rule?"

"There are a couple who haven't, but it causes a scandal."

"How bad can a scandal be?"

"I don't know. I've never been involved in one. But it's not good for your reputation. People might not invite you to their dinner parties, or they might forbid you from going to a ball."

"Do you go to any dinner parties or balls now?"

Ignoring the twinge of embarrassment she always felt when she considered all the things she never did, she said, "No. The truth is, I don't do much of anything except stay home. It's been like that since my mother died. I have a brother who visits when he's not busy doing his job, but until I met you, I haven't done anything."

"Then why does it matter if my cousin is your suitor or not? What harm will come to you if people find out?"

None, Eris supposed. Who knew if enough people even knew who she was? She might not even make it into the *Tittletattle*, and if she did, who would decide they would stop talking to her?

"I can't see denying a love match no matter what the cost would be," Reina continued. "It makes no sense to worry about what other people think when you don't even associate with them to begin with."

Reina was right. It didn't make sense. And it wasn't like Jonathan was going to come back. The vicar had made it clear that her marriage vows would be void if Jonathan died. It was unfortunate it'd happened so soon. But should she deny herself the opportunity to fall in love with someone who was interested in her if she had the chance at a love match? Jonathan had been a nice person.

She couldn't imagine that he'd expect her to remain a widow forever if she could be happy with someone.

Maybe she shouldn't be so quick to dismiss Mr. Duff's attentions. Maybe Reina was right. Maybe he did enjoy being with her. Maybe the things he'd said and the kiss he'd given her were more than something he'd done to be polite.

Her heart gave an unexpected flutter. What did it matter what others thought? If she had another chance at marriage, she'd do well to take it.

Eris hesitated to reply, but after a moment, she admitted, "I think there are some things more important than what the Ton has to say. No one has to live with the consequences of your decisions but you, right?"

"Exactly! If my cousin asks to be your suitor, I hope you'll say yes. He's a kind and sweet gentleman. I just know he'll give you that love match you've been longing for."

Eris didn't know how to respond, but fortunately, she was saved from having to come up with something since Reina started talking about things she was looking forward to doing in London.

Chapter Six

"When you ask to be Eris' suitor, she'll say yes," Reina told Charles later that day as the two played cards in his townhouse.

He had suspected Reina hadn't been merely bored when she came over to see him. He knew she had planned to go for a walk with Jonathan's widow earlier that day. He had intended to pay her a visit tomorrow to find out if she had asked the lady if she'd be open to a romantic relationship with him, despite the fact that such a thing would be scandalous. He didn't know how far she was willing to go in her role of the grieving widow. Now he knew she didn't even care enough about Jonathan to give him the year's mourning his passing deserved.

And why should she? She killed him. Why should she care about his legacy enough to remain without a suitor, or a lover, for a full year? For all he knew, she already had a lover on the side.

Charles selected a card and put it down. "You and the Duchess of Jowett must be getting along wonderfully if you're referring to her so informally."

"You might as well refer to her as Eris," Reina said then sipped her tea. "That's how I think of her. She and I became friends right away. I can't thank you enough for introducing me to her."

"I didn't exactly introduce you two."

"Not in person, but you did lead me to her townhouse and told me what to say."

He shrugged. Yes, he supposed one might consider that to be an introduction, though he wasn't sure he would. But that was beside the point. The truth was, he was surprised the two were getting along as well as they were.

He lowered his gaze to the cards. He wasn't sure how he felt about this unexpected turn of events. He never meant for Reina to be friends with Eris. That complicated things. When he finally exposed Eris for killing Jonathan, Reina was going to be devastated.

Charles cleared his throat and looked at his very happy and naïve cousin. She was such a trusting soul. It would be best if he didn't wait much longer before making Eris think he had fallen in love with her. The sooner he got Eris to marry him, the sooner he could look through that townhouse without arousing her suspicions. He was sure the evidence he needed was in that place. It was just a matter of finding it. Then, once he made sure justice was achieved, he'd be here to comfort his dear cousin.

"Since Eris is willing to live under the shadow of a scandal, I suppose there's no reason I can't let her know how I feel," Charles finally said.

Reina looked up from her cards and squealed in delight. "I was hoping you'd say that! This is so romantic. She wants a love match so much. She thought she was going to get that when she married your friend, but, as we both know, his untimely death stopped that. She didn't think she was going to get a second chance. Now she will. I just love how I got to be a part of this. You two are such nice people. You both deserve to be happy."

He forced himself not to wince. Yes, she was much too trusting.

"Let me know the next time you'll go for a walk with Eris, and I'll happen to show up," he said.

"I'll do that," she replied, not hiding her excitement. "I can't wait."

She was definitely going to be devastated when he exposed Eris for the person she really was. He just hoped he could find a way to make this up to his cousin.

***

"I don't think I'll ever get tired of these walks," Reina said two days later. "Hyde Park is just gorgeous!"

"Wait until the flowers are in bloom," Eris replied. "It'll look even better."

"No, it can't look better than this." Reina glanced at a bush that currently had no flowers on it. "Can it?"

"You'll see for yourself when the time comes. Although, I will say it's a very pretty park to go through even in winter."

And it was better when she had someone to walk with. It was nice to be a part of the activities in London. She was starting to forget how it felt to be stuck home all day now that she and Reina had developed a friendship.

"Why, I don't believe it," Reina said as she tapped Eris' arm. "My cousin didn't say anything about taking a walk today."

Eris followed the lady's gaze and saw Mr. Duff heading in their direction. All at once, warmth wrapped around her, and her heart gave an unexpected leap. She glanced at Reina, hoping she didn't notice the effect he had on her. She took a deep breath in an attempt to steady her nerves.

"My dear cousin," Reina said as he approached them. "I didn't know you were coming out here this afternoon. If I had known, I would have invited you to join us."

"I was on my way home from seeing a friend," Mr. Duff replied. "I wasn't planning to come this way, but I thought I'd take advantage of the nice day."

"I don't blame you," Reina said. "Eris and I were just talking about how nice it is out. In fact, it's why I asked her if she wanted to take a walk. Why don't you join us?" She glanced at Eris. "You don't mind, do you?"

"No, I don't mind," Eris replied, secretly hoping he'd say yes.

"Since neither of you object, I'll be happy to walk with you," he said.

Eris couldn't be sure, but she thought his gaze lingered on hers a bit longer than necessary. She could only hope that people would assume her cheeks were pink from the chill in the air instead of the thrill that swept over her. She'd never experienced anything like this before. She'd had the beginnings of it with Jonathan, but it had never been able to go anywhere. Perhaps this time might be different.

"So who did you visit?" Reina asked her cousin.

"Lord Draconhawthshire," Mr. Duff replied.

"You're jesting," Reina said.

"No, I'm serious. That's his title."

Reina chuckled. "That's quite a title. One could write a book with something that long."

"He didn't choose the name of the title," Mr. Duff said. "It was passed down from his brother to him."

"One would need to see it written down to know exactly how it's spelled," Reina insisted. "I don't know why all titles can't be easy to spell; or remember, now that I think about it." She glanced at Eris. "My cousin's father is Lord Jackman. Jackman is easy to spell, and it's easy to remember. I don't know how anyone is expected to remember something like Dracon-another-word-or-whatever-ahire."

Eris could tell Mr. Duff didn't find Reina's attempt to repeat his friend's title amusing, but he politely said, "Draconhawthshire."

Reina shrugged. "As long as you can remember it, that's what really matters. I just hope his Christian name isn't equally long and complicated. His poor wife will have a terrible time of it if not."

"You'll be happy to know his Christian name is Eric," Mr. Duff replied.

"Eric what?" Reina asked.

"Eric is it," he said.

Reina's eyes grew wide. "His name is Ericisit?"

Eris bit her tongue so she wouldn't laugh. It was apparent to her that Reina was intentionally messing up the gentleman's name, but her cousin seemed oblivious to the game.

"No," Mr. Duff said. "His name is Eric. That's it."

Reina tapped her lips for a moment. "Ericthatsit. Lord of Dragon-halfway-up-a-hill-or-tower-or-higher."

Mr. Duff didn't hide his exasperation. "You can't be serious."

Wishing to help the poor gentleman, Eris said, "She's teasing you." Glancing at her friend, she added, "You're a bit of an imp."

Reina laughed. "I know it's wrong to tease my dear cousin, but he takes everything so seriously. My other cousin—that is his oldest sister—told me he doesn't know how to joke around." She put her hand on his arm. "Forgive me. I shouldn't embarrass you. I was only having fun."

It was then that Eris noticed how red Mr. Duff's face was.

"Is his name really Eric?" Reina asked.

"Oh no, you're not going to drag me into this again," Mr. Duff said.

"I wasn't going to tease you about it this time," Reina replied. "I was only going to say that his name is so much like Eris'. Can you imagine if he were to marry her? They would be Eric and Eris."

"Well, he is looking for a wife," Mr. Duff said. "He's only twenty-three, though. I told him he has plenty of time, but he's insistent that he marry soon."

"Not everyone wants to wait as long as you," Reina replied.

"I know that," Mr. Duff began, "but he's convinced he'll die on his twenty-fifth birthday."

"If he thinks he'll die so early, then why even marry?" Reina asked.

"For an heir. It's why most gentlemen marry." His gaze went to Eris. "I, however, prefer love to be my reason for doing so."

Surely, he wasn't hinting at his attraction to her. Eris must be making more out of his words than were really there.

Maybe there really is something there, and you're too scared to admit it.

Eris bit her lower lip. It was possible fear was preventing her from seeing what was really there. But what if he was only making conversation? Just because he wanted to marry for love, it didn't mean he was attracted to her.

She stuffed her hands into her pockets and forced her attention to the other people who were at the park.

"I'd like to meet this friend of yours," Reina said. "I don't suppose you'll invite him over for a dinner party and let me be there."

"I don't know," Mr. Duff slowly replied. "You find his name and title so amusing that you'd probably laugh at him."

Her eyes grew wide. "I would never do anything like that to him in person. That would be terribly rude. I might not have grown up in London, but I know how to be nice to people."

"Why do you want to meet him?" he asked.

"I'm curious about why he thinks he'll die when he turns twenty-five."

"You can't ask him about it."

"Why not?"

"Because it's none of your concern." He shook his head. "I never should have told you."

"I find it fascinating that someone would think he's doomed to die on his birthday. He's not sickly, is he?"

"No, he's in perfect health."

"Then why is he convinced he'll die?"

"I don't know, and quite frankly, I don't think we need to know. This is something personal. If he wanted me to know, he'd tell me."

"Have you asked him?"

"Why would I ask him about it?"

"Because you're his friend, and as his friend, you don't want to see him die. Maybe it's something you can prevent."

"How can I stop someone from dying if he's doomed for death?"

"Maybe there's some spell that's been cast over him," Reina said. "Maybe a grandfather clock is going to fall on top of him on his birthday. If you knew that, you could spend the day with him and make sure he stays away from all grandfather clocks."

Mr. Duff rolled his eyes in exasperation, and Eris had to agree that Reina's reasoning was absurd. "He's probably just scared he'll die on his twenty-fifth birthday," Eris intervened, hoping she might do something to help the situation.

"Yes," Mr. Duff agreed. "I think that's it, exactly. I'm sure it's all in his mind."

"I wonder why that should be," Reina said, a thoughtful expression on her face.

Mr. Duff shrugged. "We'll never know because we're not going to pester the poor gentleman about it."

"Can I still meet him?" Reina asked, giving him a pleading look. "I promise I won't say anything about him dying when he turns twenty-five."

"Don't look at me like that," Mr. Duff said.

"Why not?"

"Because you know it only weakens my resolve," he muttered.

"But I want to see what someone by the name Dragonhawkandshire is like." He shot her a pointed look, and she hurried to add, "I was trying my best to say it correctly that time."

"You just need to separate the sounds out. Dracon-hawth-shire. Say it slowly. Dracon."

"Dracon."

"Hawth."

"Hawth."

"Shire."

"Shire."

"Put it all together," he said.

"Draconhawkshire," she replied.

He sighed. "I suppose that's the best I'm going to get."

Eris chuckled, and the two glanced at her. "I'm sorry. I didn't mean to laugh."

"I wasn't trying to mess the title up," Reina said.

Eris realized that, which was why the situation was so humorous. "Just address Lord Draconhawthshire as *my lord*," she told her friend. "You'll be fine."

"How is it that you can repeat his title without any problems but she can't?" Mr. Duff asked, not hiding his surprise.

"I picture the title in my mind when I say it," Eris replied.

"I'll address him as *my lord*," Reina told her cousin. "It's easy to do that. And I won't say anything about him dying when he turns twenty-five. I'll be good."

Mr. Duff nodded. "All right. I'll host a dinner party at my residence." His gaze went to Eris. "Would you be willing to join us?"

Not hiding her surprise, Eris asked, "You want me there?"

"Well, this way it would be even. My friend can escort my cousin to dinner, and I can escort you. Then we can play games like charades or cards," he replied. "It'll be a lot more fun to play with four people instead of three."

Reina gave Eris an excited look that she knew for a fact meant that Mr. Duff had to be interested in her in a romantic sense. Otherwise, why would he make it a point to pair Reina up with his friend while pairing himself up with her?

Ignoring the thrill that coursed through her, Eris said, "I'll be happy to attend the dinner party."

"I'm glad we'll be together," Reina replied. "This will be so much fun! I can't wait."

Eris couldn't wait, either, but she was too afraid to say it. This all seemed like some kind of dream. She couldn't believe this was really happening, and to her of all people. Her brother hadn't had to arrange this dinner party for her. Mr. Duff had invited her himself.

Maybe, just maybe, she was going to get the love match she'd always wanted.

Chapter Seven

"I hope you don't mind that I stopped by unannounced," Charles said as he entered Eris' drawing room the next day. "I thought my cousin might be here." That was a lie. He knew full well that Reina was shopping with his mother, but he had to come up with some excuse in order to see Eris. "She was talking about coming by to visit you. I assumed she meant today." He offered an apologetic smile. "I can see that I was wrong." He gestured to the book Eris was holding. "My apologies. I won't keep you from your book."

As he hoped, Eris said, "You might as well stay and have some tea since you came all the way over here."

Pretending to think it over, he said, "I don't want to disturb you."

"You're not disturbing me. I can read this later." She slipped a clip into the book to mark her place. "Take off your coat and hat and have a seat."

He turned to the butler and handed the servant his hat and coat. Afterward, he opted to sit on the settee. He could have chosen a chair, he supposed, but it wouldn't allow him to suggest she sit next to him. If he was going to play the part of the besotted gentleman, the settee was his best choice.

He noted that she told the butler to bring the same things he'd had the last time he was here. Jonathan's cook made excellent scones. It was no wonder she served those so much. Jonathan used to eat them a lot. He cleared his throat and forced his friend from his mind.

After the butler left, she went to the chair she'd been sitting in when he arrived.

"You can sit with me," he said before she sat down. "There's plenty of room on the settee." When she hesitated, he added, "I'll be escorting you at my dinner party. We might as well get comfortable with each other."

A slight blush colored her cheeks before she sat beside him.

"That wasn't painful, was it?" he teased her.

"No, of course not. We're just sitting."

"Precisely." He paused then added, "It's good practice. We'll probably end up sitting next to each other on the settee at my townhouse. My cousin and friend will meet for the first time tomorrow. It's best they sit in chairs. I doubt she'll find him to her liking."

"Do you mind if I ask why not, or is that too personal?"

"You can ask. Reina is a lady full of laughter and joy. I'm sure you've noticed that."

Eris nodded. "Oh yes, she's a lovely person to be around."

"I enjoy my friend's company. I wouldn't be friends with him if I didn't. But he has a tendency to be somber. It's his fear of facing an early death that does it. He's very intelligent. I suspect he's smarter than most in London. Nevertheless, that fear has dimmed his enthusiasm for life. I suppose if I believed I was going to die soon, I might not be such an enthusiastic person, either."

He glanced at her, wondering if she would try to kill him the same way she'd managed to kill Jonathan. Well, let her try. It'd be easier to prove she'd murdered his friend if she did. Unlike Jonathan, he would be careful around her.

Clearing his throat, he continued, "I can't think of two people more different than Reina and Eric. The most I can hope is that they'll have a pleasant evening talking and playing games." He laughed and touched her arm. "Forgive me. I was so caught up in sitting next to you that I forgot to tell you that the dinner party is tomorrow."

Her eyes grew wide. "Tomorrow?"

"I know it's soon." He smiled but removed his hand from her arm lest he seem too forward. "I hope you don't mind me saying it, but I was impatient to see you again. Had I known I was allowed to spend some time with you today, I would have had the dinner party later on in the week. Do you forgive me?"

"It's not a sin to have a dinner party so quickly because…because…"

When she failed to finish the sentence, he realized it was because she couldn't bring herself to admit what he was trying to get her to believe.

"Yes, I confess my intentions are that of a romantic nature," he whispered in a way he hoped would convey sincerity. "I told myself it was best to wait. I really don't want to seem impatient. My friend hasn't been gone for long. I realize it's not appropriate for you to entertain suitors so soon. It's just that," he paused on purpose as if he was struggling with what to say, "you didn't know Jonathan very well, and you weren't even married to him beyond a day. Also, Reina told me you didn't have time to fall in love with him."

Eris winced.

"Jonathan told me about you," he hurried to add. "He said you were beautiful and kind. He spoke of you in such a way that made me envy his good fortune." He cleared his throat. "I don't think anyone expected you to be in love with him. The marriage was arranged, and you two were chaperoned up until your wedding day."

"Yes, that's true," she replied.

They grew quiet, and Charles felt a surge of panic well up within him when he realized he had run out of things to say. He couldn't very well suggest they elope. Yes, that was his goal, but he couldn't get to it so soon.

The time wasn't right. She had to be fully convinced he was in love with her first.

Thankfully, the butler came in and set the refreshments on the table.

As the butler left, he thought of something to say that wouldn't press the issue of romance. "Tell me about your family."

"Well," she began, "my brother and I are all that's left."

She picked up the teapot, and he noticed that her hands were trembling as she poured tea into their cups. A subconscious admission of guilt, perhaps? Had his reminder that she hadn't loved Jonathan disturbed her? Was it possible she experienced a slight sting of conscience over ruthlessly killing him?

"My father died when I was six, but he left us with money," she said. "We never wanted for anything. My mother passed on a couple of years ago."

"She never married again?" Charles asked.

Eris shook her head, and he noted how attractive she was with those dark curls framing her face. He supposed Jonathan thought the same when he used to look at her. She really did appear harmless. His poor friend would never have suspected that she was a wolf in sheep's clothing.

She set the teapot down and held a cup out to him, her hand still a bit shaky. "I'm not sure my brother will ever marry. He doesn't have the kind of life that would make for a good husband. He's always going from one job to another, and he works at all hours."

Charles accepted the cup. "Plenty of gentlemen have jobs that require them to be away from home at different times of the day."

"Yes, but his job comes with some danger, too."

Charles took a sip of the hot tea. "I suppose that makes sense. I bet your brother has a lot of interesting stories to share."

"Probably, but he doesn't share them. What about your family? I know Reina's staying with your parents, and there was a mention of you having a sister."

He drank his tea as he debated how much to tell her. He had to let her get close to him, but he couldn't let her get too close. After a moment, he said, "I have three, but only one is old enough to have a husband, and she's married with a child and another on the way. She's excited about adding another member to the family."

"I can't begin to imagine what it's like to expect a child."

He wondered if she might be expecting a child right now but telling him. Jonathan's dead body hadn't been discovered until the morning, and the doctor estimated the time of death to be anywhere from ten in the night to one in the morning. Jonathan could have consummated the marriage then returned to his bedchamber where he met his fate.

Maybe she'd managed to slip poison into his drink without him finding out. Or maybe she had offered him something to drink in her bedchamber and the poison didn't take effect until he was back in his own bed. Not all poisons worked immediately.

He glanced at the cup he was holding. For a split second, he wondered if he had been careless to drink from it, but then, he remembered the butler had brought the tea, and he had watched her pour the tea into his cup. She hadn't had an opportunity to slip something into it.

Besides, why would she? She wasn't married to him. Jonathan was just fine until his wedding night. Charles relaxed. He didn't have to worry yet. The time to worry was after he married her. The only chance he had of finding the proof he needed to convict her of murder was by getting full access to this townhouse.

Eris bit into her scone. "Are you and your sisters close?"

"The oldest has her own life with her husband," Charles replied. "I see her from time to time, but usually, it's when we have something special happening in the family. As for the other two, they're still children."

"My brother is my closest friend. I don't know what I'd do without him."

"That's nice." It must help to have someone in the family whose job it was to track down criminals when one was a killer. If her brother discovered what she'd done, he'd probably do his best to make sure no one else found out.

She bit into a piece of the scone, and a crumb fell to her gown. She hurried to pick up one of the cloth napkins and searched for it. He hesitated to point it out to her since it had landed between the edge of her gown and her breast. Fortunately, she shifted as she continued looking for it, and it ended up in her lap. That was a much safer place to point to.

"It's right there," he said, gesturing to it.

"Thank you." She picked the crumb up with her napkin and set the rest of the scone on the tray. She offered an apologetic smile. "When I'm nervous, I can be clumsy."

Nervous, or guilty? Pretending to believe that it was a simple case of nerves, he said, "You have no need to be nervous around me. I very much enjoy your company."

A blush crept up her face as she folded the napkin, and put it on the tray.

"I hate to leave, but I still need to find my cousin," he said when he couldn't think of a single other thing to say.

"Oh, I forgot you were looking for her."

"I did, too, but one can't blame a gentleman for being forgetful when he's around a charming lady. I'm looking forward to the dinner party." He considered kissing her cheek or her hand, but he figured he'd already taken enough liberties for the time being.

She cleared her throat. "I'm looking forward to it, too."

She began to rise to her feet, but he stopped her by placing a hand on her arm. "There's no need to get up. I'll see myself out." He let his hand rest on her arm longer than necessary then stood up. "I'm counting down the hours until I get to see you again."

As he made his way to the front door, he smiled. That had gone much better than he'd hoped. She believed everything he'd told her. He was sure of it. If tomorrow evening went as he planned, he should have no trouble convincing her to run off and marry him.

Chapter Eight

Eris' hands shook as she struggled to put her gloves on. She was even more nervous than she'd been yesterday when Charles had stopped by looking for Reina. So much could happen this evening. She was both terrified and excited at the same time.

She had spent the entire day figuring out how she should style her hair and which jewelry to wear to the dinner party this evening. After much debate, she chose to have her hair pulled up and for black pearls to decorate her hair. Since the only color she could wear was black, it'd only taken her ten minutes to select the gown that she thought might best flatter her figure.

A part of her experienced a sense of guilt over being so excited about seeing someone other than Jonathan. It wasn't fair to his memory that she let another gentleman occupy her thoughts while she was awake.

But Jonathan's not alive. It's not like you're being unfaithful to him.

And she wasn't getting younger. If she was Reina's age, she could give Jonathan the full year's mourning he deserved. But the hand of time was ticking against her. How could anyone expect her to turn down the only other opportunity she might ever get at having a love match? Was it fair that she let this chance pass her by?

She wanted to be a wife. She wanted someone in her life who would hold and kiss her and love her. She'd wanted it for the longest time. It was why she'd agreed to the marriage her brother had arranged for her.

And wasn't this better? With Charles, she already knew he desired her. She didn't have to hope that someday he might develop a romantic attraction for her.

She clasped her hands together and took a deep breath. Whatever happened this evening, she was going to follow her instincts. She wasn't going to let the rules of the Ton prevent her from being happy. This was her life. She had a right to a love match. No one else was going to live her life for her. It wasn't going to be them who had to live the rest of their lives alone without a husband or children. What did they have to lose if she didn't pursue a love match?

A knock came at her bedchamber door. On the other side, her footman said, "The carriage is ready, Your Grace."

She straightened up and retrieved her coat and hat. The evening held a lot of promise. All she had to do was be willing to accept it. She buttoned her coat, and once she could trust her hands not to shake too badly, she left the room.

The carriage ride did little to calm her nerves, but she did manage to get enough control to appear calm. Soon, she found herself at the front door of Charles' townhouse.

"Everything will be fine," she whispered. "If nothing else, you can smile and nod when the others are talking."

Feeling more at ease, she used the knocker to let the footman know she had arrived.

After a moment, the footman opened the door and invited her in.

"I'm the Duchess of Jowett," she said as he took her coat and hat. "I believe Mr. Duff is expecting me this evening."

"Yes, he told me you'd be coming tonight. I'll take you to the drawing room."

She swallowed the lump in her throat and joined him as he led her down the hall. As they neared the drawing room, she heard two gentlemen talking.

"I don't know if I like the idea of having my silhouette drawn on a piece of paper," the unfamiliar gentleman was telling Charles. "I heard that a soul can be captured that way."

Charles laughed. "Who told you something as silly as that?"

"Lord Quinton."

"That explains it. He reads far too many fanciful stories. It fills his head with all kinds of superstitions. I keep telling you not to listen to him. All he'll do is add to your worries."

When they noticed her and the footman, the footman said, "Her Grace, the Duchess of Jowett, has arrived."

Charles hurried over to her and smiled. "Splendid. I'm glad you came this evening."

What was quickly becoming a familiar warmth flowed through Eris. "I said I'd be here."

"Yes, but you might have changed your mind since I last saw you. What is your favorite tea?" he asked her.

"Black tea is good," she replied.

Charles turned to the footman. "Have the butler bring black tea."

The footman nodded, and Charles took her by the arm so he could escort her into the room. The touch sent a thrill straight through her.

"This is my friend Lord Draconhawthshire," Charles introduced. "I already told him about you."

The gentleman bowed. "It's a pleasure to meet you."

She curtsied. "It's a pleasure to meet you, too."

"Since my cousin has trouble with long names and titles, I thought we should address each other informally," Charles said. "Eric, this is Eris."

Eric's eyebrows furrowed. "Did you say Eric or Eris?"

"I know the names are similar," Charles said. "No one planned it, but this is the way things are."

"I can go by Algernon if it helps," his friend suggested. "That's my middle name."

"I didn't know you had a middle name," Charles replied in surprise.

"It's not something I tell everyone," he said.

"I don't have one," Charles replied. "I know it's becoming more popular to have one, but my parents only saw it fit to give me and my sisters one name." He glanced at Eris. "Do you have one or two names?"

"Only one," she replied. "My brother, however, knows a few people with a middle name."

"It's amazing how much you learn as you get older," Charles said. "I've been on this Earth for thirty-seven years, and I haven't met anyone with a middle name."

"That's not true," Eris replied and gestured to Algernon. "You know him."

"Yes, but I didn't know he had a middle name," Charles said.

"Now you do." Her gaze went to his friend. "I like it."

"It'll help my cousin if we call you Algernon," Charles told his friend. "She was afraid she'd get your name confused with Eris'. She also thought if she did, it would be funny." He gave a slight roll of his eyes. "She finds amusement in a lot of things."

"Perhaps a game of charades might be more to her liking than sitting around and drawing silhouettes," Algernon said. "Sometimes those can be funny. It'd be a nice distraction to laugh for a while."

Eris wondered what he meant by that, but Charles turned back to her. "Do you like charades?"

"It's been a long time since I've played the game, but I think it's fun," she replied.

"Good. Then we'll do charades." Charles put his hand under her elbow and led her to the settee.

She sat next to him, and Algernon went to a nearby chair. The butler came into the room and set the tray on the table. He left, and Charles poured tea into the cups.

"Has anything new happened since we last talked?" Charles asked her.

Though she didn't want to come out and admit she led a very boring life, she said, "No."

"Well, Algernon's had the good fortune of being accepted into White's today," Charles said. "I haven't been granted the privilege of becoming a member of the gentleman's club. It's quite an honor. He has every right to boast, except he doesn't."

She caught the teasing tone in Charles' voice and smiled as she accepted the cup he handed her.

Algernon shrugged. "My older brother was a member shortly before he died. I don't know how encouraging it is to know I've been selected to join. I'm thinking of telling them no."

Charles gave him a sympathetic look. "Your brother had an unfortunate accident." With a glance at her, he added in a low voice, "His brother died in a duel." Turning his attention back to his friend, he added, "That could happen to anyone who isn't careful about the company he keeps. It doesn't mean anything bad will happen to you if you accept the invitation to become a member of White's."

Eris noted the uncertainty in Algernon's expression and couldn't help but feel sorry for him. Charles was doing his best, but she guessed that the kind of fear that Algernon lived under couldn't be smoothed over by logic.

The footman came into the room with Reina, and Charles proceeded to make the introductions to Algernon and his cousin.

After he was done, Reina sat in a nearby chair. "My apologies for being late. I had the most difficult time selecting the right gown for this evening. I wanted something festive since we're here for a dinner party, but it had to be warm enough to overcome the chill in the room. I'm looking forward to spring."

"The gown you picked is perfect for this dinner party," Charles assured her as he gave her a cup of tea.

He settled back next to Eris, and she couldn't be sure, but she thought he sat closer to her this time.

"The rose color looks beautiful on you," Eris told her friend. "I agree with Charles. The gown is perfect."

"Yes, you are a lovely sight," Algernon added.

Reina's smile widened. "I shall choose this color more often in the future since everyone's in agreement about it."

After a few moments of silence, Charles said, "We were discussing the types of games we should play after dinner. What do you think of charades?"

"I love charades!" Reina exclaimed. "It's so much fun to guess what someone is trying to convey without using any words. I promise not to pick something too difficult this evening." Glancing at Eris and Algernon, she added, "The last time I played the game, no one figured out what I had chosen to be."

"She chose to be a bridge," Charles said. "I know such a thing sounds simple when I say it, but it's not so simple when she looks like she's trying to reach for the drapes that are on the other side of the room while she's bowing."

"I was thinking of a drawbridge," she clarified. "The kind that the king's men would lower down when someone was permitted into the castle."

Eris could see how that would be hard to guess. "Maybe we should agree to something like animals. Those shouldn't be too hard to figure out."

"But they might be too easy," Reina replied.

"That depends on how you handle acting like one," Charles said. "I don't think all animals are easy."

"As long as it's not a raven, I think animals are a good idea," Algernon spoke up.

"What's wrong with ravens?" Reina asked.

"They're bad luck," Algernon replied.

Reina's eyes grew wide. "They are?"

Charles sighed. "I wish you would stop talking to Lord Quinton. He sees misfortune in everything."

The butler came into the room and announced dinner was ready.

As they stood up, Charles added, "No one will act out a raven during charades."

Algernon didn't hide his relief.

"This is going to be a relaxing evening," Charles assured his friend. "Why don't you escort Reina to the dining room? I'll escort Eris." He glanced Eris' way in a way that made her heartbeat pick up. He placed her hand around his arm then turned his attention back to his friend. "We have much to look forward to." Without another word, he led everyone to the dining room.

***

Charles hardly paid attention to the game of charades. He suspected he had Eris exactly where he wanted her. If he took too long, she might get wise to the real reason he wanted to be with her, and if that happened, he'd lose his chance to convict her of Jonathan's death.

When it came time for the dinner party to end, Algernon left first.

"I had a marvelous time," Reina said as she and Eris got ready to leave. "I didn't know dinner parties could be so much fun."

"You don't think the ones my parents and oldest sister have are fun?" Charles asked in surprise.

"Not like this." Reina thought for a moment then shrugged. "I'm not sure how to explain it. It's just different when a gentleman who isn't married is in attendance. It gave me an idea of what having a suitor will be like."

"I like Algernon," Charles began. "He's a good friend, but he's also morbid. I'm not sure he'd be an ideal match for you."

"I barely know anything about him except that he's good at charades," she replied. "He got almost everything right."

"Yes, he is good at games like that." Probably because it was something he could do indoors, which meant it was a safe activity. Charles decided not to voice the thought aloud.

"Well, thank you for letting me come," Reina added. "I'll see you both soon."

"Maybe we should go to our carriages together," Eris said as she slipped her hands into the pockets of her coat. "I must be going, too."

"Actually," Charles spoke up, "I would like a moment alone to speak with you, if you don't mind."

Reina shot an excited look in Eris' direction, and he pretended not to notice it. Up to now, his cousin had been subtle, but he was afraid Eris might figure out Reina was a part of his plan if she wasn't more careful.

A blush created a nice pink hue on Eris' cheeks. "I'll see you tomorrow," Eris told Reina.

"Or a little later than that," Charles hurried to add.

Reina's eyes grew wide.

He waited for Eris to glance away from him before he mouthed, *I'm going to ask her to marry me. We might elope.*

Reina managed to suppress her enthusiasm and settled for telling Eris, "Just send me a calling card when you're ready to see me."

Charles released his breath as she hurried out of the room. He scanned the doorway and was glad to see no servant lurking nearby. Now it was time to act.

"Eris," he said as he directed his gaze to her, "I can't tell you how much I enjoyed the evening with you."

"I enjoyed it, too."

The tone of her voice hinted at her shyness. She looked shy, too. If he didn't know better, he'd believe she was incapable of murder. It was no wonder the doctor and constable didn't give serious consideration to his insistence that Jonathan had been murdered.

Well, he knew better. She was a killer, and he was going to prove it.

He drew her close to him and tucked one of his fingers under her chin. He lifted her face toward him and kissed her. He didn't make it a habit of kissing ladies, so he reasoned that it was normal for a gentleman's heart to speed up with pleasure while doing this. It also had a peculiar way of making him feel warm and tingly all over.

When the kiss ended, he whispered, "This evening doesn't have to end."

"But the dinner party is over."

"While that's true, we don't have to say goodnight."

She gave a slight wince. "I'm not comfortable going to a gentleman's bed unless he's my husband."

He had expected that to be the case. After all, she couldn't inherit his money unless he was married to her. "Marriage is what I have in mind. Run off with me to Gretna Green. We'll leave tonight."

"But…but…isn't this all sudden?"

"It is, but I can't deny how I feel. From the moment I saw you, I was enraptured by you. I thought I was going to have to spend the rest of my life pining for you. Now that I have the chance to be your husband, I don't want to waste it. Complete me, Eris. Be my wife."

She hesitated to reply, and he suspected the rational part of her mind was prompting her to say they needed to take things slower. There wasn't any reason why they had to rush this.

With Jonathan, she'd been able to plan everything out. She was probably thinking that she needed more time to plan out his murder so that she could get away with losing two husbands instead of one. He couldn't allow her to gain such an advantage.

He brought his mouth back to hers, and this time he continued kissing her until he felt her relax against him. She wrapped her arms around his neck. In response, he deepened the kiss. Good. This was perfect. He had her exactly where he wanted her. Reason had left, and in its place was passion.

"Will you go with me to Gretna Green?" he whispered once the kiss ended.

All of her resistance had fallen away. She nodded and said, "Yes, I'll go with you to Gretna Green."

Chapter Nine

Eris didn't sleep at all that night. This had to be the most reckless thing she'd ever done. Her brother would be appalled if he knew that she was running off to Gretna Green. She wasn't sure how she was going to adequately explain why she agreed to such a hasty marriage. Charles had kissed her, asked her to marry him in the sweetest way, and then kissed her again until all she wanted to do was be with him forever.

Once she had packed enough things to get her by for the next few days, she joined Charles in his carriage, and the two rode out of London. He had held her and gave her more kisses. Then they had grown silent, and at some point, he had fallen asleep.

Sleep eluded her, though. The whole evening had been so much like a dream. She never thought something like this could happen to her. Imagine a gentleman taking an immediate liking to her but thinking he'd never have the chance to be with her. No one had ever held her up in such a romantic light before. There was no way she could deny this chance.

She hoped Jonathan wouldn't think she'd had no intention of being faithful to him. She had. Her plan had been to be only his, and while she had hoped children might result from the union, she had wondered if her age would work against her. She wasn't young like most ladies were when they married. They had plenty of child-bearing years left. Despite that, she had hoped to give Jonathan an heir. It was a shame she couldn't have done that much for him. But what could be done about it now? It wasn't like she could go back in time and invite him to her bedchamber earlier in the evening.

From the brief time she'd known Jonathan, he had struck her as a gentleman who would have understood why she was going to marry again so soon. Also, Jonathan had been Charles' friend. Charles spoke so tenderly when he talked about him. Jonathan must have been even more wonderful than her brother had made him out to be for Charles to have held him in such high esteem. She didn't think Jonathan would hold any ill will toward her for rushing to marry again. If she'd been the one who had died, she would have wanted him to find happiness.

She looked out the window and glanced up at the sky. The moon was quickly setting. Soon, the sun would be coming up for the day. She did believe in a life after this one, but she often wondered if those who passed on to that next life could see what was happening down here.

From beside her, Charles stirred. She turned her gaze to him and saw that he was waking up. Her heartbeat picked up, and she shifted in the seat so she could face him. Her foot hit her valise, and she leaned down to move it out of her way. She straightened back up and dared a peek at him. She wasn't familiar enough with him to feel comfortable about openly staring at him.

She loved looking at him. He'd been blessed with strong male beauty. She couldn't understand what it was that had attracted him to her. She'd spent her entire life as a wallflower. No one had ever noticed her without her brother's assistance. But Charles had. There must be something about her that convinced him she was worth pursuing.

Her skim warmed with pleasure. It was a wonderful feeling to know one was desired by a gentleman.

Charles jerked up.

Her eyes widened in surprise.

"I didn't realize I fell asleep," he said as he struggled to blink the sleep from his eyes.

"I didn't mind," she assured him in case it embarrassed him. "The ride has been a nice one."

He glanced at her. "Did you sleep at all?"

She shook her head. "I tried, but I couldn't." Feeling a bit shy, she added, "I'm too excited by everything. I don't think I could sleep even if I was in a bed."

He settled back into the seat and smiled. "It is exciting. We have a lot to look forward to." He reached out and took her hand in his. "I woke up in time to see the sunrise. It'll be nice to share this moment with you. Have you seen a sunrise before?"

"No, actually I haven't."

"It's splendid. There are few things in this world as beautiful as a sunrise. I especially love the colors. The pinks and oranges of the morning chase off the blue of night. Then the sun makes everything go back to blue, but this time the blue is a nice light color."

"It sounds lovely. I'm sorry I never took the time to pay attention to it before." And it wasn't like she hadn't had time to. She'd just never been inclined to wake up early. "I tend to wake up around nine. The sun's already up by then."

"Well, you're up now, and more importantly, you're with me." He moved closer to her and gave her a kiss. "I figure we'll stay at an inn this evening. We should get to Gretna Green tomorrow. Then we'll be united in marriage."

"I can't wait."

"I can't, either. Everything will be exactly the way I want them to be after we marry."

She had to refrain from giving away just how excited she was. It was fine to let him know how much she was looking forward to being married to him, but she didn't need to jump up and down in the carriage like someone who'd never had anything this exciting ever happen to her before. Love was turning out to be so much better than she'd dreamed possible.

Charles put his arm around her shoulders and motioned to the window. "What do you think?"

She directed her attention to the window and saw the sun peeking out from the hills in the distance. As he'd said, the colors in the sky were breathtaking. There was nowhere else she'd rather be than with him in this moment.

"Every time I look at a sunrise from now on, I'll think of you," he whispered in her ear.

Her smile widened. She just might make it a habit of waking up early every day so she could look at more sunrises, for she'd love nothing more than to think of him as well.

***

That evening when the coachman brought the carriage to the inn, Charles breathed a sigh of relief. Acting the part of the besotted gentleman wasn't easy when one had to do it the entire day. Beyond a few breaks to take care of personal matters, he'd had to keep up the façade.

But Eris seemed to believe everything he was telling her, and that was the important thing. As long as she didn't pick up on the fact that this was all a ruse, he'd be able to follow through with his plan.

The first thing he needed to do was inspect Jonathan's bedchamber. While she might have been careful enough to avoid everyone else's suspicions, there might be some clue hiding somewhere in that room. Or, if no evidence presented itself, he might get lucky enough to catch her in the act of trying to kill him. Of course, given how he would rather not die, his main hope was that there might be proof in Jonathan's bedchamber. She was, after all, very clever. He might not succeed in outwitting her if she were to make a move to kill him.

Charles forced his attention back to the lady who had, finally, dozed off beside him, thereby allowing him some time to plan what he should do tomorrow after they married. He had to be careful. Everything had to be planned out.

"Eris," he said as he softly shook her. "It's time to wake up." Her eyelids fluttered, and he gently shook her again. "We arrived at the inn."

She straightened up and yawned. "I'm surprised I fell asleep."

"You didn't sleep at all last night, and you were awake until an hour ago. I'm not surprised sleep caught up with you."

The coachman opened the door.

Charles took her hand. "Come along, my dear. We'll have something to eat and then have a good night's sleep. Then we'll be refreshed for tomorrow."

He led her out of the carriage then took their valises. They entered the inn, and soon, they each had their own room.

"I'll have someone bring your food up to your rooms," the innkeeper told him.

Turning to Eris, Charles said, "I'll bring my meal to your room so we can eat together."

Charles figured that a gentleman in love would prefer to eat dinner with his lady rather than eat it alone. Even though he was tired and wanted nothing more than to have a quick meal and go to sleep, he didn't dare give up the pretense.

Once he was in his room, he opened his valise to make sure Eris hadn't taken anything out of it or put anything in it. The chances of her doing anything to hurt him was slim at the moment. He probably had to worry about her after they exchanged vows, but it never hurt to be careful. Now wasn't the time to let his guard down. He had to remember what happened to Jonathan. The stakes were much too high.

When he found that his valise was just as he'd packed it, he relaxed. Good. She hadn't done anything yet. He was still safe for the moment. He put his hand over his heart and relaxed against the table.

After he set his things away for the night, a knock came at his door. At first, he thought it might be Eris, but then a woman called out that it was the innkeeper's wife.

He answered the door, and a woman who held a covered tray was waiting for him. "I brought you your meal, Mr. Duff. I'll be coming up with Her Grace's meal in a moment."

"Thank you."

He took the tray but waited until she was going down the steps at the end of the long hall before he brought the tray into his room and set it on the dresser. He lifted the cover. Everything looked all right. He should be safe eating this. And the glass of wine should be safe to drink.

He released his breath, set the cover back over the plate, and carried the tray to Eris' room. He intended to knock on Eris' door, but the door was already open. That was surprising for a lady who thought nothing of murdering her husband. One would think she would know better than to leave her door open like this. She might as well invite someone to come in and do something horrible to her.

He knocked on the door to let her know he was there.

She turned from the table she was setting for their meal. She smiled when she saw him. "I was just about to bring the chairs over to the table." She waved for him to enter.

He stepped into the room and glanced at her valise. She hadn't taken anything out of it. He wondered what she had chosen to bring along. If he'd been smart, he would have looked inside it while she was asleep in the carriage.

No, that wouldn't have worked. The valise had been between her feet and the carriage wall. He probably would have woken her up. Then she'd know that he suspected her of murdering Jonathan. It was better he hadn't looked through it.

He placed his tray on the table as she brought the chairs over. The innkeeper's wife came in with her meal and set it next to his. Eris closed the door after she left.

He shook his head. Now she thought to close it?

She returned to him. "I'm so hungry I'd eat anything, but our meals smell delicious, don't you think?"

He lifted the lids from their trays and set them aside. "Everything does look good. It's much better than the bread and cheese I brought along for us to eat during our trip here."

They both sat down, and she offered him an apologetic smile. "I didn't mean to imply I didn't appreciate the things you brought for us to eat and drink."

"You're much too kind. Those things aren't nearly as good as a full meal." He picked up the glass of wine and held it up to her. "To the most desirable lady in all of London."

She blushed with pleasure and tucked a strand of hair behind her ear in a manner that indicated bashfulness.

He was impressed with how well she could act. She put some of those actors at the theatre to shame.

They ate for a while in silence. At the dinner party, Reina had done most of the talking, which saved anyone else from having to come up with something to say. Without his cousin there, he was stuck having to come up with a way to start the conversation. He could go on and on about Eris' beauty, he supposed, but he didn't dare push his luck. If he paid her too many compliments, she'd grow suspicious. Being in the carriage, all he'd really had to do was comment on the scenery, hold her, or kiss her. He'd even used the occasion to discuss what they would likely do at Gretna Green once they got there. He wasn't sure what else he could say at this point.

Eris cleared her throat, and he looked up from his meal to her. "I didn't think of this before, but will I be moving into your townhouse after we return to London?"

"Actually, I thought it might be best to move into yours."

Her eyebrows furrowed. "I thought gentlemen preferred it if the wife moved in with him."

"Yes, that's usually the case, but Jonathan was my friend. I still miss him." He always would. "I like thinking of him and being surrounded by his things."

"I wish I had gotten a chance to know him better. From the way you talk about him, he must have been a wonderful person."

"He was. There are very few like him." Before the conversation got too serious, he swallowed the lump in his throat. "He would have been happy with this arrangement." Especially since he knew Charles would do the right thing and expose her for the person she really was.

"I'm relieved to hear that. To tell you the truth, I wondered how he'd feel about it. He and I had only shared a few conversations, and except for the ones right after the wedding breakfast and at dinner, my brother was with us. He and my brother did most of the talking. I sat by and listened. I know more of him than I actually knew him."

"He died so suddenly. How could you have gotten the chance to know him?" It took all of his willpower to leave the bitterness out of his voice as he said those words. He took a sip of his wine. "The townhouse is all either of us have left of him." He paused. "Unless, of course, you end up with his child."

Her face turned a brighter shade of red. "No, unfortunately, that's not possible. We never consummated the marriage."

"You didn't?"

"No. I waited for him to come to my bedchamber, but he never did."

She lowered her gaze, and she was spared the sharp look he gave her. She'd been so eager to get rid of him that she'd murdered him before he even had a chance to conceive a child?

Charles forced the question aside. She could be lying. But if she was telling the truth, it was better no child would be on the way. What child would benefit from having a mother who was a murderer? The poor child would suffer shame and humiliation every day of his life.

Charles had arranged for there to be no child between them. One of the things he had made sure to pack in his valise was a sheath. There was no way he would bring a child into the world with a lady who murdered his friend. He planned to wait until he married again before trying for an heir.

"I left all of Jonathan's things in his bedchamber," Eris said after she took a sip of wine. "I wasn't sure what to do with them. It would be best if you handled those items. You know what he would have wanted to do with them. Perhaps he has a relative who might want those things. I assume you'll want to use his bedchamber."

"Yes, I do want to use his bedchamber."

He wondered just how much she had left untouched. He hadn't gotten the chance to see Jonathan's bedchamber. If she hadn't gotten rid of anything, then that would be ideal. But, of course, she'd certainly taken time to get rid of anything connecting her to the murder. The doctor and constable had been to Jonathan's bedchamber, and the constable had assured Charles that he'd searched it, though Charles often wondered if he'd searched it good enough.

"I'm relieved you'll figure out what to do with his things," she said.

He didn't know if she was telling him the truth or not, but if anyone was to handle Jonathan's personal things, it should be someone who actually cared about him. "I'll make sure Jonathan's things are taken care of when we return to London," Charles replied before he turned his attention back to the meal.

Chapter Ten

The next evening, Charles and Eris arrived in Gretna Green, and the first thing Charles did was secure two rooms at the inn. He then told Eris he'd come to her room once he washed up. This gave him time to memorize where everything was in his room. If she ended up sneaking in here at some point, he had to know about it. After he married her, he was going to be like a gentleman who was trapped in a den with a lion.

If someone had told him a year ago that he'd be doing this, he would have laughed. He'd spent his entire life avoiding anything that would place him in a dangerous position. Safety and security had been the tenets he had lived by, and they had served him well. But there came a time when a gentleman had to take a risk. This was his time.

Once he checked his reflection to make sure he looked like an eager bridegroom, he left his room, careful to shut the door.

He took a moment to compose himself. He didn't like the fact that his hands were shaking. The gloves hid this for the most part, but he could still feel it.

He closed his eyes. *I'm doing this for Jonathan. When the truth comes out, this will all be over.* He didn't believe in restless spirits roaming the Earth, but he fancied the idea that Jonathan might find contentment up in Heaven once people knew Eris was a murderer.

A calm came over him, and Charles went up to Eris' door and knocked on it.

A few seconds passed before Eris opened the door. She had taken time to brush her hair and pull it back into a flattering style. He pretended he didn't find her attractive. The last thing he wanted to think about was how pretty she was. While it was going to make going through with the consummation of the marriage easier, it was a betrayal to his friend's memory to get any pleasure from what he was about to do.

"The innkeeper has arranged for a priest to marry us after we eat," he said. "I thought we'd eat downstairs this time." So that she wouldn't get suspicious, he added, "The meal will go faster if we don't have to wait for someone to bring it to us."

"That's fine with me," she replied as she stepped into the hallway and shut her door. "I'm so nervous. I'm not sure I can eat anything."

Yes, he supposed plotting the death of one's husband would ruin a lady's appetite. "I'm sure you'll be able to eat something. It's a long way to morning."

Especially when one had to worry about whether he'd see another sunrise.

Poor Jonathan. He never did see another morning. Charles pushed the thought down, offered her a smile, and escorted her down the stairs.

Charles ended up indulging in more sweets than he could ever remember having at one time, but he reasoned a gentleman risking death could afford to forgo the healthier options. Eris, however, barely ate more than the potatoes and small slice of roast duck.

After they were done eating, they went to the blacksmith's shop. Charles had heard elopements could be expensive, and sure enough, the anvil priest charged him a substantial fee to perform the wedding. It was a good thing Charles managed well with his finances.

He paid the fee then joined Eris at the anvil where the ceremony occurred. Charles didn't really pay attention to what the man was saying. For all he cared, the man could have been talking about the weather. This whole marriage was a farce. With any luck, Eris would be imprisoned within a month, and Charles could put this whole thing behind him. When the ceremony was done, the man struck the hammer on the anvil and congratulated them.

"It always warms my heart to unite a couple in holy matrimony," he said.

Charles suspected the man's heart warmed much more from the outrageous sum of money he'd just made but figured there was no point in saying that. If his plan worked, the money would be worth it.

Charles thanked him then escorted Eris back to the inn. There was only one thing left to do that evening before he could finally go to sleep and put this day behind him, but he found his resolve wavering. Jonathan had been murdered on his wedding night. From this moment forward, Eris had the right to his money. She could kill him anytime to get it.

He stopped at her room and said, "I'll visit you in a bit. I have something I need to do before I'm ready to be with you." When he noticed the way she frowned, he asked, "Is something wrong?"

"No, of course not. It's just…" She bit her lower lip and fidgeted.

"It's just what?" he prompted.

"Well, a part of me worries that I won't see you again. The last time I saw Jonathan alive, he said the same thing." She let out an uneasy laugh and adjusted her hat. "It's silly to worry something like that will happen again."

His eyebrows rose. Had Jonathan gone to his bedchamber and she'd followed him to enact her plan? "I won't be long." Then, so she wouldn't feel the need to follow him, he gave her a quick kiss and opened the door to her room. "Make yourself comfortable."

She offered him a nod and stepped into the room. He gave her a wave then shut the door. He stepped back and waited to see if she would come out, but she didn't.

Releasing his breath, he hurried to his room and shut the door behind him. He leaned against the door for a few moments while he gathered his courage. He could do this. He *would* do this. And he would be just fine as long as he was diligent. Jonathan hadn't known she was a murderer. He hadn't been paying attention to what she'd been doing. But Charles would pay close attention to everything she did.

Once he felt ready, he went to his valise and took out the pouch that was holding his sheath. He put it aside then took out his robe. While he didn't relish the idea of going down the hall in only a robe, there was no way he was going to stay in her room all night. He wanted to get some sleep.

Reminded of going to sleep, he returned to the door and made sure there was a lock on the handle. Good. This innkeeper put locks on the rooms. Once Charles returned to this room, Eris couldn't slip in and kill him while he slept.

He removed his coat and then his clothes. He slipped the pouch into his pocket. His hands were still shaking. This wasn't good. He didn't like this. He was much too nervous. He was never going to be able to relax enough to consummate the marriage unless he did something about it.

He saw the decanter the innkeeper had left in his room. He hated the idea of drinking alcohol. It lessened the ability to think clearly. But it was relaxing, and right now he desperately needed that.

He went to the decanter and lifted the lid. He sniffed the liquid. It wasn't brandy. It was probably ale. He picked up a glass and poured a little of the ale into it. He tested it, noting its rich malt sweetness.

This would work.

He filled his glass until it was almost all the way to the top and then placed the lid back on the decanter. After taking a deep breath, he gulped the liquid down until the glass was empty. He set the glass down and took another deep breath. Already, a pleasant warm feeling was beginning to course through him. There. That should help ease his nerves.

He tightened the belt on his robe, and, with his shoulders back, he went to his door. He opened it a crack and made sure no one was in the hallway before he slipped out of his room. He hurried to Eris' room and knocked on her door, hoping she would open it before someone came out of their room and saw him. Fortunately, she was quick to invite him in.

He felt himself relax a bit once he was in her room. Good. The ale was beginning to work.

He noted that she wore a gown that must have been reserved for bed since the fabric was thin enough to give him a detailed outline of her breasts. They looked fuller in this gown than they did in anything she wore during the day. And a part of him had no trouble responding to that.

This was also good. He needed to be erect for what was coming next.

"Would you like something to drink?" she offered as she went to the two glasses that were already filled with what appeared to be wine.

The color of the liquid in her glasses was lighter than the caramel color of the drink in his room. No doubt the innkeeper brought her something with less alcohol in it.

But he wasn't going to drink it. In fact, he wasn't going to drink anything she offered him unless he saw a servant bring it in and then watched her pour it right in front of him. For all he knew, she could have slipped poison into this drink.

He shook his head when she brought the glass over to him. "No thank you. I'm not thirsty."

"Oh, all right."

He studied her. Was she disappointed?

She placed his glass back on the small table and sipped her wine. If he wasn't determined to prove she'd killed Jonathan, he would come up with a distraction so he could swap the glasses. Only then would he know if there was poison in it.

Actually, that would be a bad idea. He was alone in this room with her. If she were to die, then they'd accuse him of murder. And all of this careful planning would be for nothing.

She placed her glass next to his and turned to him. She offered him a shy smile. "You'll have to forgive my inexperience. I don't know what I should do."

He seriously doubted she was really a virgin, but he supposed he was going to find out soon enough if this was one area she'd chosen to be honest about.

"I'll lead," he told her then went over to the bed.

He pulled back the blankets, taking his time so he could search under them for any kind of weapon. Then he picked up the pillows and pretended he was only interested in fluffing them as he patted them down.

Well, there was no pistol or knife. The bed was safe. He turned his gaze back to her. Her hands were at her sides. She wasn't holding anything. Her hair was down. So he didn't have to worry about any pins. Not that he thought she could kill him with hairpins, but one couldn't be too sure. Also, there was no way she could hide anything in a gown that thin.

All right. For the moment, at least, he had nothing to worry about.

"Come and join me on the bed," he said and patted the mattress.

She did as he wished, and as she crawled into the bed, he removed his robe. This was it. The moment had come.

He removed the sheath from the pouch. Having never done this, he wondered if it was best to put the thing on before he got started or wait until he was fully erect.

He supposed waiting until he was fully erect would be best. While the ale was allowing that part of him to get excited about what was to come, he wasn't quite ready to enter her.

He set the sheath and pouch on the small table by the bed and turned to her just as she lifted the gown over her head. Well, that was all he needed to become fully aroused.

He took the sheath off the table and slipped it on, making haste to tie it in place at the bottom of his shaft before she noticed. Once she was settled onto the bed, he took the blankets and pulled them up to their waists.

His gaze went back to her breasts. They looked much better close up. He brought her into his arms, noting how soft they were when they were pressed against his chest. He didn't know if it was the ale or holding her naked body that was making him forget about his apprehension about being with her, but the last of his unease departed.

He brought his mouth to hers and kissed her. Kissing her while they were naked in bed was much more enjoyable than kissing while they had their clothes on.

She wrapped her arms around his neck and pulled him closer to her. Encouraged, he prompted her to open her mouth to him. She obeyed his leading, and his tongue brushed hers before he explored her mouth in earnest.

He pulled her closer to him and traced her back and behind. Her skin was much softer than he'd expected, and while he had noted her curves when she was dressed, they were much better to touch than to look at. He brought his hand up to one of her breasts and cupped it in his hand. He didn't think it was possible, but his erection grew harder. That was good. Now he'd have no trouble consummating the marriage.

His mouth left hers, and he kissed her cheek and then her neck and left a trail of kisses all the way down to her breasts. He spent considerable time exploring them. He fancied himself as someone who appreciated the beauty of art, but nothing was as lovely as this.

He would spend all evening just taking delight in those lovely breasts if the male part of him wasn't so impatient. He hadn't taken care of the baser part of his desires in quite a while, and that was quickly catching up to him.

He urged her to part her legs and then settled between them. He gave her another kiss before he entered her. He noted how tight she was, so he instinctively grew still and waited for her to adjust to him. Had it not been for the fact that the sheath dulled some of the pleasure from being inside her, he wouldn't have been able to do this, but the sheath turned out to be useful for this specific moment. She might not have thought anything about murdering his friend, but he didn't exactly relish the idea of hurting her.

At least he knew for sure that there was no way she could be carrying Jonathan's child. She had most definitely been a virgin.

When it was impossible for him to remain still anymore, he pulled gently halfway out of her and then eased back into her. She relaxed, and he repeated the movement a couple of times, doing his best not to go any faster than she could tolerate. After a while, she wrapped her legs around his waist and pulled him deeper into her. All reason left, and the only thing he could do was give into the need for release. And when the release came, he let out a low moan and spilled his seed.

Once he was done, he collapsed in her arms. He'd never felt such an incredible sense of relief and peace wash over him before. He thought it had to be the ale fully taking effect, but in the back of his mind, he wondered if this was a natural result of being with a lady in such an intimate way. He had overheard gentlemen saying there was no greater pleasure than making love to a lady. This could very well be why.

He had no idea how long it took before he could move, but when he did, he was overcome by the urge to look at her. She really was a beautiful lady. Even with her clothes on, she was worth admiring.

He couldn't resist the need to kiss her. In this case, he reasoned it had to be the ale making him behave so amorously. Alcohol had a way of lowering his guard, which was why he was careful to limit how much he drank at any time, even when he was among family and friends. His life was all about control and order, and he'd seen too many gentlemen succumb to things they shouldn't because of excessive drinking. He had drunk much more ale than he should have this evening, but it had been necessary. Now that he had consummated the marriage, the deal was done.

He lingered for quite some time at Eris' lips before he finally pulled out of her, careful to keep the sheath securely to him. The temptation to stay in the bed and hold her or talk to her for a while was there, but it was best not to stay here too long. He was starting to feel sleepy. If he ended up falling asleep, who knew what she'd do?

"I should get back to my room," he said as he removed his sheath. He noticed the trace of blood on it, offering further confirmation about her virginity.

"Do you have to?" she asked. "I wouldn't mind it if you stayed."

He was sure she wouldn't. He'd already gotten further with her than Jonathan had. His poor friend.

His resolve strengthening, he said, "We have a long carriage ride tomorrow. It's best that we get a good night's sleep." So that she didn't get suspicious, he looked at her and smiled. "I want to be alert during our ride. I don't want to sleep through a single moment we have together."

She returned his smile. "I don't, either."

He tried to resist kissing her again, but the ale was too strong. He leaned toward her and brushed his lips with hers. "I'll come by first thing tomorrow morning," he said.

That seemed to satisfy her since she didn't protest as he got up and slipped on the robe, making sure he was discreet when he put the sheath and pouch in his pocket. Knowing she had been a virgin made him reluctant to be overt about showing her things that ladies of ill repute probably saw all the time.

He wished her a good night's sleep then went to his room.

Chapter Eleven

Eris supposed she should be tired, but she had trouble sleeping that night. She was much too excited to sleep. It had to be love. She'd never been in love before, but this had to be what it felt like. When Charles was with her, she felt like all was right with the world, and when he was gone, she missed him terribly. He stirred up feelings of hope and joy she hadn't ever experienced before. And if that was due to love, then she concluded love was the most wonderful experience in the world.

Finally, she was able to drift off to sleep, and she didn't wake up until someone knocked on her door. She reluctantly stirred from her slumber, but when she realized it was well past dawn, she hurried to put on her robe so she could answer the door.

Charles glanced at her robe in surprise. "I thought you'd be up and ready to leave by now."

Her face warmed. "I can be ready in ten minutes. Do you mind waiting a little longer?"

"No, I don't mind. I'll tell the innkeeper to bring us something to eat and have it delivered to my room. Come when you're ready."

"I'll do that."

As he turned to go back to his room, she shut the door. She hurried to wash up and get dressed. The only thing that took her more time to get ready than it should have was deciding how to wear her hair. She wished she knew how Charles preferred ladies to style their hair. She'd choose that hairstyle. She supposed it didn't matter. She was going to wear a hat to cover her head anyway since they were going to spend most of their day in the carriage. After she pulled her hair back into a bun, she put on her boots.

She put the coat over her arm then gathered the valise. When she got to Charles' room, the door was ajar. She tapped on the door and peered into it. He was putting the chairs at a table.

He glanced her way and his eyes widened in surprise. "You're actually ready?"

She chuckled as she stepped into the room. "I said I would be ready in ten minutes."

"I have a mother, three sisters, and a cousin who say they can be ready in ten minutes but end up taking a lot longer than that. When I point out how much longer they take, they only say I can't expect a lady to rush. You have just proved them wrong."

"I don't know what to say." Maybe some ladies took a while to get ready, but she'd never had trouble with being quick.

He came over to her and took her valise and coat. "If I were to tell them I have proof a lady can get ready in ten minutes, I don't know if they'd be disappointed or if they'd be upset with you for revealing the truth." He offered her a smile that made her entire body flush with pleasure. "I think this will be our secret."

"Yes, that's probably best," she replied as he hung her coat by the door and set her valise under it. "They don't have to know that you know the truth."

"No, they don't." He placed his hand on the small of her back and led her to the table. "The cook is making waffles and poached eggs. I hope that's all right."

"It's perfect."

Everything during this entire trip had been perfect. For the first time in her life, she was getting the thrill of knowing what it was like to have a love match. He could have said they were going to eat porridge, and she would be happy.

She sat in a chair, and he helped push the chair in for her.

"Are you looking forward to returning to London?" he asked.

"It will be nice to see your cousin and my brother." Her eyes lit up. "We can invite them over for a dinner party."

He sat across from her. "I thought your brother was busy with his work."

"He is, but there will be a time when he's between jobs." She sensed his surprise and asked, "What?"

He shrugged. "I don't know. I assumed you had no intention of introducing me to someone whose job it is to solve crimes."

She laughed. "My brother's job has no bearing on whether or not I'd introduce you to him. Of course, I want you two to meet. You're both important to me."

He didn't answer right away, and when he did, he said, "That's actually nice."

Someone called out that the meal was ready. Charles jumped up from the chair and opened the door. The innkeeper's wife came in and placed the tray on their table. Eris placed the napkin across her lap but waited until Charles returned to the table before she began eating.

***

As soon as they entered her townhouse, Charles told the footman, "Have my things brought here. This will be my new residence."

Eris waited until they were alone in the drawing room before saying, "Are you sure you don't want me to move to your townhouse? Just because you said that's what you wanted on our way to get married, it doesn't mean you can't change your mind."

"I still want to live here." He drew her into his arms and smiled. "You don't mind it if I move in here, do you?"

"No, of course not. If you want to be here, that is fine. I should ask the maids to clear the bedchamber for you, though."

He stopped her before she could leave his arms. "There's no need for that. I'll take care of Jonathan's things. Besides, it'll be nice to have his things around me."

Noting the pain in his voice, she hugged him. "I'm sorry. I wish you didn't have to go through the pain of losing someone so close to you."

He hesitated to return the hug, and she reasoned it was because he was a gentleman and gentlemen weren't known for expressing their grief. So as not to make him uncomfortable, she pulled away from him.

"I think I'll go upstairs," Charles said. "I'd like to get an idea of where I'll put my things."

"I'll show you to the bedchamber," she offered.

"There's no need to do that. I know where Jonathan's bedchamber is. He showed me around the place after he first got it. I won't be long. I only want to know where I should tell the coachman and footman to put my things."

"Oh, all right." She smiled. "You probably know more about this place than I do. So far, I haven't ventured much beyond my bedchamber, the drawing room, and the dining room."

The butler came into the room with a tray of tea and crumpets.

Charles gave her a light pat on the small of her back. "Why don't you sit and pour us both some tea? I'll return to you shortly." He gave her a quick kiss then headed out of the room.

She turned to the butler and thanked him as he left. She went to the table in front of the settee and poured tea into the two cups.

The footman came into the room. "Your brother wishes to visit. Should I let him in?"

"Yes, bring him in!" She put the teapot down and hurried to the doorway just as her brother was about to enter the room. "Byron!" She hugged him. "I'm so happy to see you."

He returned her hug then led her further into the room. "I'm glad to see you're all right."

"I'm doing fine. I eloped."

"Yes, I know."

She didn't hide her surprise. "How could you know? I left at night without telling anyone."

He urged her to sit on the settee and settled next to her. In a low voice, he said, "I'm a Runner. It's my job to figure things out. You weren't here when I came by the other day, and word around London is that Mr. Duff went missing at the same time. Then I recalled Mr. Duff was a friend of Jonathan's." He shrugged. "It was easy to piece everything together. But Eris, are you sure rushing into marriage to someone neither one of us knows was a good idea?"

"I know him. He came by soon after the funeral to ask if he could have something of Jonathan's. I gave him Jonathan's cane. I thought that was going to be the end of it, but it turns out he is the cousin of a new friend I made. So we got to know each other better, and we ended up falling in love."

His eyebrows furrowed. "It's a strange coincidence that he happens to be the cousin of a friend you just made."

"I think it's more than a coincidence. I think God took pity on me after Jonathan's death and gave me another chance at a love match. Oh, Byron, Charles is just wonderful. He's kind, sweet, and attentive. We get along so well. I hesitated to marry so soon after Jonathan's death, but I'm not getting any younger. A lady my age doesn't get many chances. I hope others in London will understand."

"People in London care mostly about themselves," Byron replied. "They'll talk about this for a while, but the gossip will quickly be replaced with something else." He accepted the cup she offered him.

"I don't care what others say. I did worry that my actions would upset Jonathan, even though he's no longer alive."

"Jonathan wouldn't hold any ill will against you for wanting to be happy, Eris. That's not the person he was. He was a decent, honorable gentleman. That's why I arranged for you to marry him."

Hearing her brother's words only confirmed what Charles had told her, and that eased the last of her discomfort about marrying so soon. "I never would do anything to hurt Jonathan or his memory."

"I know you wouldn't. You're not that kind of person."

"Are you happy for me?"

"I'm happy that you're happy. I only hope it lasts."

Some of her enthusiasm waned. Why would he say such a thing? "Do you think I made a mistake?"

"I don't know what to think yet. I have to get to know Charles. I only met him once, and that was for a brief moment. I knew Jonathan, and he was someone I trusted."

She let out a chuckle. "You can trust Charles. He's a lot like Jonathan. Besides, why would Jonathan be friends with someone who isn't trustworthy?"

Her brother shrugged. "I'm sure Jonathan trusted him."

"Well, there you are. That's the answer we both need. And I know Reina. She's Charles' cousin. She's a delightful person. I should have you over for a dinner party. You can get better acquainted with both of them."

"I would like that."

"Good. A dinner party will be fun."

Someone entered the room, and they directed their gazes to Charles. She jumped up from the settee and ran over to him.

"I have good news," she told Charles. "My brother came by for a visit." She took his hand and led him to the settee where her brother was rising to his feet. "Do you remember him?"

"A little," Charles said. "Jonathan introduced us."

Her brother nodded. "Yes, and that wasn't all that long ago. I happened to notice that my sister was back in London and thought I'd find out where she'd run off to. I was beginning to think she disappeared."

"I explained to him that we married," she told Charles. Then, looking at her brother, she added, "We went to Gretna Green."

"It sounds romantic," her brother replied.

"It was," she said. "Everything was perfect. I can't think of a better trip. Charles, would you like some tea?" She picked up the cup she hadn't taken a drink from. "You can have this. I'll summon the butler to bring in another cup."

"That's not necessary," Charles replied. "I'm not thirsty. You should have it."

"You two should sit on the settee since you're married," Byron offered as he went to a nearby chair.

After they sat, Eris said, "I invited my brother to a dinner party. We can invite Reina and anyone else you wish."

"A dinner party is an excellent idea," Charles replied.

"Good," Byron said. "I'd like to get to know you better."

"I look forward to that, too," Charles replied.

Eris smiled. It was nice to see Charles and Byron together. Who knew? Maybe they might become friends.

The three grew quiet, and after a minute, Eris gestured to the crumpets. "Is anyone hungry?"

"No, I'm not," Charles replied.

Well, she was hungry. They hadn't had anything since breakfast that morning, and that was eight hours ago. She picked up a crumpet then glanced at her brother.

"I'll have one," her brother said.

She gave one to him then began to eat hers.

"What do you do?" her brother asked Charles.

"Do?" Charles replied.

"For work," Byron clarified.

"I invest," Charles said. "The profits I earn make me a comfortable living." He paused. "Eris told me you're a Runner."

Byron nodded. "Yes, but I have to wait until there's some crime or suspicion of a crime in order to get hired. I make just enough to get by. I don't have the luxury of spending time investing."

Charles stiffened. "What I do is work. I don't sit around and play card games all day or run off to dances or the theatre at night."

"My apologies. I didn't mean for my comment to come out the way it did," Byron said. "I only meant that with how busy I am, I can't make connections with other gentlemen to find out the best businesses to invest in. My job takes me all over London, and sometimes even outside of it. There's also no consistent schedule. I'm up at all hours of the night part of the time."

Eris noticed Charles relax and felt the tension leave her body. Though she hadn't been directly involved in the conversation, she hoped things would remain pleasant. She couldn't blame her brother for being shocked. She'd be shocked, too, if her brother left London for a week and returned with a wife. It was even worse that she hadn't had a chance to tell him that she was falling in love with Charles before she left. How was he supposed to be prepared for this? Even she was still adjusting to everything that had happened.

"Byron," she began, "I'm glad you came by. I would have introduced you to Charles earlier, but you weren't in town. At least we have now and the dinner party. And, of course, we have the rest of our lives. I have no doubt that you two will be friends soon enough."

She glanced between the two gentlemen and noted that while her brother remained expressionless, Charles gave a slight flinch. She frowned. Perhaps she hadn't done anything to make the awkward situation better. It might have been better if she'd kept her mouth shut.

"I'm sure you're right, Eris," her brother said. "Since Charles and I both liked Jonathan, I see no reason why we won't get along." He paused then added, "It might be best if I give you two some time alone. I just wanted to make sure you're all right. A brother can't help but worry about his sister, even if she is older than him."

She gave Byron a smile and stood up with him. "I'm glad you came by. I know this came as a shock. I promise not to do anything else to shock you."

Her brother chuckled. "Good. In my line of work, there are surprises that come up, but that doesn't involve my sister." He gave her a friendly tap on the back then turned to Charles. "I look forward to talking to you again."

Charles, who had gotten to his feet as well, offered a pleasant smile. "We'll have a good time."

At once, Eris felt better. Maybe things would be all right after all. She joined them as they went to the front door. As the footman opened the door, she saw that Charles' carriage had returned, and the coachman was pulling a trunk from it. Another servant was gathering another trunk.

"I better show them to the bedchamber," Charles said before he headed down the steps of the townhouse.

Byron turned to her. "He's moving here?"

"He said he'd rather do that than have me move to his townhouse," Eris replied.

"Did you ask him to move in here?"

"No."

Her brother nodded but only said, "Let me know when you'll have this dinner party."

"I will."

He smiled then put his hat on his head and left the townhouse.

Since she didn't want to get in Charles' way, she decided to go to her bedchamber and put her things away.

Chapter Twelve

Charles collected all of the objects Jonathan had owned and put them in the small room off to the side of the bedchamber so they would be easy to go through in the future. The clothes were of little consequence. There would be no clues in there to lead him to solving the murder. He wasn't sure what to do with them at the moment, so he had instructed a servant to bring an empty trunk and put Jonathan's clothes into it.

But with everything else, he was going to go through those items as time permitted. He still had to play the doting husband, and he couldn't do that while spending all of his time in the bedchamber. So for the time being, all he could do was order the butler to send for a locksmith as soon as possible. Then he unpacked his things.

He hadn't brought everything from his townhouse. He figured it was only going to be a month or two before he got the evidence he needed to convict Eris of the crime. Then she'd be arrested, and he could return to his townhouse with the knowledge that the truth of Jonathan's death had been exposed.

Once Charles had all of his clothes and grooming supplies set in place, he changed his clothes for dinner. He was eager to finally eat. As Eris had pointed out, it had been a long time since they'd had breakfast. He was famished. Not famished enough to accept any tea or food that Eris offered him, but famished enough to eat anything the staff served. He trusted Jonathan's staff. They'd been under Jonathan's employment for years, and Charles had attended plenty of dinner parties with his friend to be familiar with them.

He let out a heavy sigh as he tied his cravat. He'd give anything if Jonathan was going to be having dinner in that dining room tonight. He glanced at the cane his friend used to own. It was propped up against the dresser close to him.

After a moment, he decided to take it with him. He wouldn't mind having something of Jonathan's with him during the meal. He took the cane and went to the door connecting his bedchamber with Eris'. It was a shame there was no lock on the door. If Jonathan had put one in, he would have been spared from her coming in here that fateful night.

Charles tested the door and opened it a crack. "Eris?" he called out.

The room, however, was empty.

A knock came at his bedchamber door. "The locksmith you requested is here, Mr. Duff," the butler called out.

Oh good! Charles was afraid he was going to have to wait until tomorrow for the man to show up. Charles shut the door and hurried to let the locksmith into his room.

The locksmith installed a lock on all of the doors in Jonathan's bedchamber. Charles felt much better. One couldn't be too safe. Afterward, the locksmith gave Charles the key, which Charles slipped into his pocket before paying him.

When Charles finally got to the drawing room, the butler was telling Eris that dinner was ready. He hadn't realized he'd been upstairs for so long.

"Are you ready to eat?" Eris asked him.

He was going to respond, but his growling stomach beat him to it. His face warmed in embarrassment.

She chuckled and took his arm. "I'll take that as a yes."

Choosing not to draw any more attention to his stomach, he said, "I hope you didn't get bored waiting for me."

"No, I was reading a book."

"Oh? What do you read?"

"Comedy."

"Comedy?" He was sure she was the type of person who'd read something darker, like the gothic fiction he'd heard about. Though he'd never read those books himself, he'd heard gothic fiction was filled with all kinds of topics like poison, murder, and hiding things. Those books were perfect for the criminal element.

"I like to laugh," she said. "It makes the heart feel lighter."

"If you say so." It was rather cold that she felt so little of murdering his friend that she could read something lighthearted, but he had to expect it. After all, did murderers even have a conscience?

They reached the dining room and sat in their respective seats. The food placed in front of him took his mind off of the grim reason that had brought him into this marriage with her.

During the meal, he asked Eris more about the books she read, but he only paid half attention to her as she described them. He wasn't much of a reader unless he could learn something from the book. Books, after all, were a means to learn something new. Fiction wasn't like that, and as a result, he saw little use for it. But he realized a lot of people found value in wasting their time this way. Even Jonathan read fiction once in a while.

After dinner, they went to the drawing room. While he was anxious to start going through Jonathan's things, he couldn't just run off to his bedchamber. He had gained Eris' trust. She sincerely believed he was interested in her. Though she might be plotting to kill him, she didn't suspect that he knew it, and that gave him an advantage. What he needed to do was hold onto that.

They played cards for an hour and a half, and they spent most of the time planning out the dinner party they were going to have. He was sure she had no intention of letting him live that long if she could manage to sneak poison into his drink or food, but she sure did talk as if she planned to let him live. She even smiled at him in a way that threatened to draw him toward her. As a result, he had to keep fighting off the urge to let his guard down.

When it was late, he walked her to her bedchamber and wished her a pleasant night's sleep before he kissed her. He had to resist the urge to kiss her too long. He was quickly learning that kissing her too long in a private setting such as the hallway in front of their bedchambers brought up certain desires he'd rather not think about. While he had managed to consummate the marriage, he had no plans to be intimately engaged with her again. Consummating the marriage had merely been a way to convince her that he wanted a real marriage with her.

All during their trip, she hadn't pressed him to come to her bed, but on this night, she asked him, "Would you like to come to my bedchamber?"

Unfortunately, there was a part of him that prompted him to say yes. It was just his luck that she was so good at playing the innocent widow.

Knowing that Jonathan's things were waiting for him gave him the strength he needed to resist temptation. "I wish I could, but the trip was exhausting." He caressed her cheek in hopes that she wouldn't start to realize his real reason for marrying her. "You're very beautiful, Eris. I'm forever grateful you agreed to elope with me."

She smiled. "I've never been happier."

"Me neither." He gave her another kiss, making sure it wasn't one that was going to weaken his resolve. Then he opened the door to her bedchamber. "I'll see you in the morning."

She offered him a nod, wished him a good night's sleep, and then went into her room. He closed the door and proceeded to go to Jonathan's old bedchamber. The maid had come up to light the candles for him, so he checked the room to make sure nothing was there that shouldn't be. While he couldn't imagine any servant who'd kill for her mistress, one couldn't be too sure. He was close now. The truth would soon be revealed. This wasn't the time to take anything for granted.

He closed the door of Jonathan's bedchamber then locked it. He checked the lock on the door connecting the bedchamber with Eris' and was reassured it was still locked. Good. For tonight, at least, he was safe.

He took a candle with him and went to the small room where Jonathan's things waited for him. After setting the candle on the desk, he scanned the items. There wasn't much to go by. There was a fob watch, a ring, and a silver cup.

He picked up the watch and turned it over in his hand. He had seen this watch a lot over the years. Jonathan had a peculiar habit of pulling it out of his pocket almost every half hour to glance at it. The chain holding it was old. Charles had once asked Jonathan why he didn't get a new chain, and Jonathan had told him that the chain had belonged to his grandfather. His father had inherited it, and then he had taken it after his father's death. "It's a good luck charm," Jonathan had mused.

Some good luck charm. It hadn't done anything to prevent Eris from killing him. Charles let out a heavy sigh and put it down.

He went to the ring next. Jonathan's father had given it to him as a gift when he turned twenty-one. It was one of the finest crafted rings in London. Or at least Charles thought so. He knew so little about jewelry. He went to the cup next. Jonathan's grandparents had gifted him the cup when he was born. It was to celebrate his birth.

Charles had to wipe the tears from his eyes. He hadn't realized that going through Jonathan's prized possessions was going to be so difficult.

Once he composed himself, he turned his attention to the drawers and searched through them. There was parchment, containers of ink, and a couple of quills. In the last drawer at the very bottom was a small book.

He took out the book and opened it. It was a list of places Jonathan had been to, including the day and time he was there. He even wrote down any people he came in contact with. Charles noted that his name was written down quite a bit. That didn't surprise him. He and Jonathan were good friends. The last time Charles showed up in the book was on Jonathan's wedding day when he had attended the ceremony and wedding breakfast.

A couple of weeks before the wedding, Jonathan had come over to tell him he was getting married. Charles had expressed his surprise that Jonathan would rush into a marriage, but Jonathan had assured him that he had met the lady and that her brother had arranged the marriage between them. Jonathan had also added that plenty of people had marriages arranged for them, an argument Charles couldn't protest.

If only Charles had fought harder to convince his friend not to go through with the marriage.

Charles let out a defeated sigh. He had searched the bedchamber. There was nothing he had gained from it. He slammed the book shut and put it back in the drawer. There was nothing he could do. Not at the moment anyway.

He shook his head. There was nothing that pointed to the murder. He'd been sure that Eris would have left some clue behind. No matter how careful someone was, there had to be a clue, didn't there?

When he realized he would get no answers tonight, he got ready for bed.

Chapter Thirteen

"I can't believe you ran off to elope," Heather said the next day as she sat across from Charles in the drawing room. "And to a lady recently widowed!"

Charles urged his sister to keep her voice down. The servants didn't need to overhear her. "A little decorum wouldn't hurt," he told her. "You need to practice some restraint."

"You ran off to Gretna Green with Jonathan's widow, and you're telling me to show restraint?"

He shifted uncomfortably in the chair. "Jonathan wasn't even married to her for more than a day."

She crossed her arms and shook her head at him. "If I had done something like that, you would have come after me and dragged me back to London." Her eyes grew wide. "Come to think of it, you did exactly that. You went all the way to Gill's estate and forced me to return to London."

He rolled his eyes. "Are you ever going to forget that? I thought Gill didn't want to marry you. He gave me no indication that he was secretly hoping you'd kidnap him."

"You didn't give me or Gill a chance to explain the situation. That's why it upset me so much. All you did was rush to conclusions."

"Yes, I'm aware of that." Again, he rolled his eyes. Just how long was she going to remind him of that one little incident in his otherwise pristine past? "I can't go back and chance any of it. Why mention it every time we're together?"

"I don't mention it every time we're together."

"It sure seems like it."

The maid came into the room and set down the tea and crumpets. Charles waited until the maid was gone before he poured tea into their cups.

"I didn't even know you were in love with Eris until Reina explained why you went missing," Heather said. "Mother and Father were appalled. They're doing everything possible to keep this scandal from spreading all over London."

"I'm surprised they're more shocked by what I did than you kidnapping someone. I didn't force Eris to go with me. She willingly joined me."

"Gill hadn't just lost his first wife, and even if he had, it's more acceptable for a gentleman to marry right away than for a lady to. What if Eris is carrying Jonathan's child?"

"She's not."

"How can you be sure?"

"He died on their wedding night before they had time to…" His face warmed, and he struggled with how to continue.

Fortunately, that wasn't necessary since his sister's eyebrows rose. "Did Eris tell you this?"

Yes, that was a safe way to proceed. He'd rather say that than to tell his sister the evidence of Eris' virginity had been too obvious to miss. "Yes, she did."

"Can you trust her to be honest about it?"

"Why would she lie about something like that?"

His sister paused as she thought over the question. "Well, I suppose there wouldn't be a reason she'd lie about it. But are you sure? The constable wasn't sure exactly when Jonathan died, and a titled gentleman's first priority is to have an heir."

"I just know." Charles picked up his cup and settled back into the chair. When he caught the skeptical expression on her face, he groaned. He was going to have to say more than he wanted to on this subject. The most he could do was be as vague as possible. "There are certain things a gentleman can tell when he's in bed with a lady. As a lady, you don't need to know what those things are. You'll just have to trust me on this."

"All right," she slowly said. "I believe you. But if she gets with child too soon, people are going to question if she's having your child or Jonathan's. That can complicate things."

"I already have that situation accounted for." When she opened her mouth to ask him how he was doing that, he held his hand up to stop her. "There are things a gentleman can use to make sure a lady doesn't get with child. I don't wish to go into any more detail than that. You're my sister, and this isn't something I want to continue discussing with you." He took a drink of his tea.

Her eyes grew wide. "Are you using a love letter?"

He nearly spit his tea across the room. After he managed to swallow most of it, he hurried to wipe his chin with the cloth napkin. He set his cup on the table. "Why can't you let things go? Why do you have to keep bringing up issues I'd rather not discuss?"

"I said the words 'love letter'," she whispered. "I wasn't going to use the real word for it. I was being discreet."

"I blame Gill for this," he said. "Before Gill came along, you were a prim and proper lady. Now you speak as if you were brought up in a brothel. I've had enough. I won't tolerate this speech anymore. If the next thing you say is inappropriate, I'll have the butler escort you out of here."

He waited, sure she was going to test him, but she only shrugged and took a sip of her tea. He breathed a sigh of relief. Sometimes his sister was impossible. It was no wonder she had practically been the death of him when she eloped.

Someone came into the room, and he glanced over in time to see Eris. He hurried to his feet and gestured for her to join them. "Eris, this is my oldest sister, Heather. Heather, this is Eris."

"I remember you from the wedding and funeral," Eris said as she reached Charles' side.

"It was a shame what happened with Jonathan, but I am glad you found a second chance with my brother," Heather replied.

"Yes, it's been a bittersweet time," Eris said.

Charles pulled a chair closer to his and urged Eris to sit. After she did, he gave her a cup of tea and then sat next to her.

"I don't remember if I told you this," he began, "but my sister is married with a four-year-old son, and she has another one on the way." Charles hesitated to give Eris the names of Heather's husband and son since he didn't want Eris getting too close to his family. It was bad enough he had gotten Reina involved in this mess.

Heather chuckled. "You don't need to be so formal, Charles. My husband is Gill Easton. He's Viscount Powell. And our son is Timothy." She took a bite of her crumpet then added, "Have you met the rest of the family yet?"

"We only got back to London yesterday afternoon," Charles hurried to tell his sister. "There hasn't been time."

Heather's eyes grew wide. "You married her without at least introducing her to our parents first?"

"They were at the funeral," Charles said. "Granted, there was no formal meeting, but they've seen her."

"I was there that day, too, and I don't recall meeting her directly."

"Well, you're meeting her now," Charles replied. "The others will meet her after we've had time to get used to being married. You and Gill didn't come over for a dinner party until you were married for six months."

"That's because you were impossible to deal with."

He shook his head but decided not to say anything in hopes she would grow bored and stop pestering him about the past.

"If you wanted to spend all of your time alone with Eris, you should have taken her to the family's country estate," she added.

"I have too many investing opportunities to do that," Charles said.

"Then there's no reason not to at least introduce her to our parents." Heather, looking much too happy, took another bite of her crumpet.

Charles sighed, but Eris chuckled. When he looked at her, she said, "I'm sorry. I tried holding the laughter in. It's just fun to watch you two."

Maybe to someone who wasn't in his position it was funny. To him, it was annoying.

"I think Charles is right about waiting for a while before I meet everyone in his family," Eris said. "Our marriage happened so suddenly. I'm sure it's going to take everyone time to get used to it." She paused. "But I am well acquainted with Reina. Your cousin is a very sweet person."

"At least Charles introduced you to someone in the family," Heather replied.

"Eris and I got acquainted when I came by to see if I could have something that belonged to Jonathan," Charles said. "Eris was kind enough to let me have his cane."

Heather's mood dimmed a bit. "I remember that cane. He took it with him almost everywhere. I'm glad you have it now. He would have wanted that."

Charles thought so, too. After a moment, Charles continued, "Eris met Reina by accident. I had arranged to meet our cousin at the market, but she insisted on walking there, and during her walk, she got lost and ended up coming here."

"It's true," Eris added. "It was chilly that day, and I insisted she come in to warm up before I took her to the market. Charles was there waiting for her."

Heather glanced between her and Charles, and Charles could see her trying to decide if she believed the story about the chance encounter with Reina that led Eris to Charles. It was just Charles' luck that in addition to Gill tainting his sister's innocence, he had also made her skeptical of what people told her.

"You can choose not to believe it," Charles said before she could ask any questions that would raise Eris' suspicions about him. "That is what happened. London isn't that big of a place."

Thankfully, Heather relaxed. "Yes, London is small. I end up seeing the same people wherever I go a lot of the time."

Glad she was going to accept the story, Charles breathed a sigh of relief.

"When, exactly, will you bring Eris to a dinner party so she can meet everyone?" Heather asked.

Charles took a moment to think over the question. The last thing he wanted was to have such a dinner party. Just how long would it take to find the evidence he needed in order condemn Eris of Jonathan's murder?

"I think two months would be a good time," he finally decided.

"That long?" Heather asked, not hiding her disappointment.

"There's a lot to do between now and then," he replied. "One doesn't just have a dinner party on a whim. There are things to plan out."

"Gill and I could host it," Heather said.

"That's not what I meant," he replied. Why did she have to interrupt him? The more she did that, the harder it was to convince everyone he had no ulterior motives for keeping Eris away from the rest of his family. "Eris and I have a lot to learn about each other, and I'd rather that happen without the rest of the family interrupting us."

Heather groaned but accepted it. "All right. Two months it is then." She finished her crumpet. "I should go. I don't want to take up too much of your time. I really only came by to see if Reina was telling the truth. I thought for sure she was wrong since you're the most cautious person I know."

"I knew Eris better than you knew Gill when you married him," Charles pointed out. "Also, Jonathan had met her and said good things about her. I know Jonathan wouldn't marry someone who would be a bad wife. He had good judgment." He paused then blinked in surprise. Had he really just said that?

Well, sure he'd said that. He had to make Eris think he trusted her, and since Heather was insisting he defend his actions, what else could he say? Sure, he had blurted the words out without thinking. That part was a bit alarming. But he reasoned he had gone over his plan so much in his mind that he could play out the lie without even thinking about it. Yes, that's why he had spoken with such conviction about Eris' good character. It didn't mean a part of him was wondering if Eris was innocent.

"You don't need to get so cross with me," Heather said. "I was only expressing my surprise. Usually, you plan everything out with great care. Frankly, I think it's good you're being more spontaneous. An elopement is perfect for someone like you. You might get more enjoyment out of life if you keep it up." She giggled and rose to her feet. "I won't keep you two any longer. I'll be on my way."

"You don't have to leave," Eris said. "We could go for a walk or play a game of cards."

"That's kind of you, but I can tell when my brother is uncomfortable, and he would like me to leave."

Charles frowned. Could his sister really tell all of her questions had made him uncomfortable, or was she making that up in order to go now that her curiosity had been satisfied?

"You're welcome to come over any time you want," Eris said. "I'd like to get to know you better."

"You'll get to know her better at the dinner party," Charles told Eris as he stood up with her. "There's plenty of time for you two to talk. There's no sense in rushing things. We have the rest of our lives for this, after all." He took Heather by the arm. "I'll escort my sister out. Then you and I can spend the day together."

Heather waited until they were out of the room before whispering, "You must really be in love to be so protective about the amount of time you get to spend with her. As you wish, I'll wait for the dinner party to talk to her again."

"Thank you," he whispered back. At least now he wouldn't have to worry about Heather complicating things. "Make sure our parents wait until the dinner party before coming over or bringing Bridget and Melanie with them."

"All right, though they'll think it's ridiculous you're waiting so long to introduce her to them when Reina's already befriended her."

As long as Heather was willing to tell their parents to wait to come over, he wasn't going to worry about what she thought about the whole thing. When it was safe to tell her the truth, she would understand.

He returned to the drawing room and saw that Eris was still standing.

"I wouldn't have minded it if your sister had stayed," Eris said. "I hope you don't think that you can't spend time with your family. I don't plan to get in your way."

"I know, but I wanted to have you all to myself." He put his arms around her and kissed her. "You can't blame a newly married husband for wanting to spend as much time alone with his wife as possible, can you?"

She smiled in a way that let him know she was flattered. "No, I can't, but I want to be certain you don't feel like you'll upset me if you want to go out and do the things you used to do before we married."

She seemed so sincere that, for a moment, he had trouble remembering why he didn't trust her.

He had to force aside the naïve part of him in order to keep a firm hold on what he knew to be true. It was no wonder Jonathan hadn't been careful around her. He would not repeat the same mistake.

He gave her another kiss. "That's very thoughtful of you, but I'm with you because I want to be." He gave her waist a playful squeeze. "Do you know how to play chess?"

"No."

"Would you like to learn?"

"I'm not sure. Is it a difficult game?"

"Not once you know the rules." He would have suggested playing cards, but he was tired of playing cards.

He wanted a different game, and though ladies weren't prone to playing chess, he saw no reason why he couldn't teach Eris how to play it. Also, chess was relaxing. With everything happening, he wouldn't mind an opportunity to relax for a while. Constantly watching everything Eris said and did could be exhausting.

"It sounds like fun," Eris said, seeming to be excited by the idea of learning how to do something new.

"Wonderful. Before the day is done, you will know how to play chess." He hurried to get the game from the library.

Chapter Fourteen

After he retired for the evening, Charles sat on the bed.

To his surprise, he was experiencing an emotion he was sure other people referred to as uncertainty. He was used to knowing what to do. While he might struggle temporarily with an issue, the answer always came to him well before the hour was up.

But for some strange reason, he now found that the war between his body and his mind could not be settled with logic. He knew it was best if he avoid Eris' bed. He'd had to consummate the marriage on the wedding night to make it official. There had been no uncertainty about what to do on that particular evening. And since then, he'd been good about staying away from her at night. It was best he avoid her. He didn't want to risk a child, nor did he want to keep up the pretense of being in love with her at bedtime.

So why couldn't he convince his body it was best if he didn't go to her again? There was no reason to go to her bed except to satisfy the baser part of him, and he had decided long ago that he'd never be given over to something as crude as lust. He'd seen how reckless some of the gentlemen in London were. Quite a few of them had lost their wits, and their fortunes, to ladies who had managed to get the best of them. He had vowed such a thing would never happen to him.

That was why he had decided to keep himself for marriage. His wife, at least, would have a responsibility to give him an heir who would one day inherit the title his father would pass on to him. And his wife would naturally be allowed access to his wealth. There was no risk of losing one's wits or fortune to a wife…so long as the wife wasn't a murderer.

He shouldn't go to Eris' bedchamber. Nothing good would come of it. He should be planning out a way to get her to expose her guilt. Sooner or later, she would reveal the truth about who she was. He just had to be patient. One of these days, she was going to do or say something that would be the clue he needed.

He let out an exasperated groan and put his head in his hands. If only his erection would go away. Late last night, he had taken care of things on his own, but it hadn't done any good. As irrational as it was, he only wanted her more.

And why not? There was nothing more arousing than a naked lady, especially one he could touch and kiss and enter.

He bolted up from the bed. He had to go to her. Things were painful enough as it was. If he didn't go to her bed tonight, he might not be able to walk tomorrow.

Even as he told himself that was an exaggeration, he found the sheath he had tucked away at the very back of a drawer and hurried to undress. He put on his robe and put the sheath in his pocket. After taking a deep breath, he went to the door connecting their bedchambers and unlocked it. So far, she hadn't tried to sneak into his bedchamber, and while a part of him did think that was odd, he had more pressing things to deal with than trying to reason through that small mystery.

He knocked on the door and called out her name.

"Charles?" came her surprised reply.

Good. She was awake. He opened the door and peered into the room. She was sitting in bed, propped up with pillows behind her back as she read a book. There were a couple of candles lit on the small table next to her.

"Is something wrong?" she asked.

"No, nothing's wrong." He stepped into the room and shut the door behind him. "I didn't know you read at night."

"I read a lot. Before I married you, I read all the time."

"All the time?"

"I love books. Some I've read at least a couple of times."

He went to her bed and sat next to her. "What kind of book are you reading tonight?"

"Nothing you would be interested in," she told him as she pulled it away from his sight.

"Why not?"

"It's something gentlemen find silly, that's why."

He found himself chuckling. "As soon as you withdraw a book and say it's silly, you do know all you've done is piqued my curiosity even more, don't you?"

"Maybe, but I speak the truth. You would not be interested in this, and quite frankly, it's rather embarrassing to be caught reading it."

She made a move to close the book, but he grabbed it from her. She gasped and tried to get it back. He, however, was faster than her and managed to turn so that she was unable to get it.

"I should have closed it as soon as you entered the room," she said, her face turning pink.

Still chuckling, he looked down at the book and read a few lines of it. He was sure it was nothing about poison or murder since she hadn't seemed guilty about reading it, and, sure enough, he was right. It was one of those sappy love stories his sister and Reina enjoyed reading. "What is it with you ladies reading stories about people falling in love?"

"I told you that you'd think it was silly. My brother says those things have no purpose in the literary world. He says it's nothing but sentimental foolishness."

Charles supposed there had to be some redeeming quality in these types of books since so many ladies seemed to be compelled to read them. He couldn't believe such books had an actual story in them. Just how complicated could love be?

But, as she had said, he had thoroughly embarrassed her, and for that, he experienced a sting of regret. There were worse books she could be reading. He, for one, was relieved this wasn't giving her ideas on how to murder him.

Hoping to ease her discomfort, he scooted closer to her and kissed her cheek. "It's not silly that you're reading this book."

She shot him a tentative look. "You don't think so?"

He should be good and give her the answer she was hoping for, but the impish part of him he hadn't listened to since he was a child insisted he say, "Someone out there took the time to write this nonsense. That is what's silly."

She gasped again, and threw the blankets over her head.

He couldn't help but laugh harder. If he had said that to his sister or Reina, they would have thrown a pillow at him. It was funny Eris hid.

Deciding to be good, he set the book on the table and moved closer to her. "I was only joking. You can't take what I said seriously. I thought you were going to hit me with a pillow."

"I couldn't do that," she mumbled from under the blankets.

"Why not? I deserved it."

"Because…because…" She shrugged. "I don't know. I just can't."

He removed the blankets from her head so he could kiss her. He let his lips linger on hers for a few seconds before he said, "I'm sorry. I didn't come in here to be difficult. Do you forgive me?"

"I could never be angry with you," she whispered, this time her face growing pink for a different reason. "So how could I forgive you?"

"You should read books that give you ideas like love. Love is much better than other things you could be reading about."

He gave her another kiss before she asked him what other things he referred to. There was no sense in bringing up anything unpleasant. He didn't feel like dwelling on unpleasant things. He hadn't laughed and joked around with someone since Jonathan died. For tonight, he'd like to enjoy the moment.

"Did I ruin the evening by making you uncomfortable?" he asked.

"No," she replied.

"Good. I'd like this to be a nice evening."

"It is nice." She put her arms around his neck. "I'm glad you're here."

He was glad, too, and surprisingly, it wasn't entirely because he needed to satisfy his more primitive side. He wasn't sure what to make of that. But he wouldn't dwell on it. He should just accept that this was a nice moment he was sharing with her. His family often told him that he had a tendency to think too much about things, and they were right. He could think tomorrow. For tonight, he was going to give himself permission to give into the luxury of simply feeling.

He brought his mouth back to hers and kissed her again. This time, he continued kissing her. She pulled him closer to her, letting him know he was welcome to be intimate with her.

He had thought he was going to be impatient. He worried that he was going to end up rushing the process, but thankfully, his desire to explore all of her made him slow down. He got much more enjoyment out of making love to her on this evening than he had on their wedding night. He was sure it had something to do with the fact that he didn't feel the need to check the sheets for a knife or some other weapon tucked away somewhere.

When he was done making love to her, he chose to stay with her. He held her in his arms and spent considerable time wondering what it might be like if it could always be like this. Such thinking was a fool's errand, of course. This marriage could never last.

He pushed the thought aside. No. He wasn't going to think tonight. He was just going to enjoy the moment. That was it. After all of the acting he'd been doing and how cautious he'd been, he deserved an evening where he didn't have to worry about anything.

Even as he told himself to stop analyzing every little thing, it suddenly occurred to him the evidence of the murder might be in this room. He scanned the area around him.

Of course! What a fool he'd been! She wouldn't be careless enough to leave evidence of the crime in Jonathan's bedchamber where anyone could find it. She would hide it in this bedchamber.

Unless she'd already gotten rid of it. In that case, he wasn't going to find anything.

But he had to search this bedchamber. He had to know if there was something here or not. He owed it to Jonathan to do a thorough investigation. The constable hadn't done his job, but Charles would make up for that.

He couldn't look right now. Yes, she had fallen asleep, but if he started rummaging through her room, she might wake up. If she saw him searching the room, she'd know that he'd figured out she had killed Jonathan. And if that happened, who knew if she wouldn't pull out a pistol and shoot him before he had time to run out of the room?

No. It was best if he didn't do anything tonight. He had to wait until Eris wasn't in this room. He had to wait until it was safe. He wasn't sure when that would be, but when the first opportunity presented itself, he was going to come in here and look around.

That still left him with tonight to allow himself to rest. Everyone needed rest. No one could spend all of their time in a constant state of planning or worrying. At some point, they had to get a reprieve. It didn't mean he was letting Jonathan down. Jonathan would tell him to renew his efforts in the morning.

Finally feeling settled, Charles closed his eyes and gave into the feeling of contentment he'd been experiencing just moments before. He stayed with her for about an hour before he finally got up and went to his bedchamber.

Chapter Fifteen

Late the next morning, Reina came by.

"I know I should have waited, but I was too excited," she told Charles as he met her in the entryway. "Heather came and told us that you and Eris returned from Gretna Green." She gasped. "Why didn't you tell me you were going to elope that night at the dinner party?"

"It wasn't planned," he whispered, glancing at the footman and hoping he was too far to overhear them. He took Reina by the arm and started to lead her to the drawing room. "I was talking to Eris, and the idea just came to me." It was a lie, but a necessary one.

"Wait! The others need to come in," Reina said, stopping him before he could take her farther into the townhouse.

"Others?" he asked in surprise.

"Your parents brought me here."

His eyes grew wide. "My parents came, too?"

She nodded in excitement. "Yes, but they made Bridget and Melanie stay home. They didn't want to overwhelm Eris. Heather said you didn't want too many of us to come by."

That wasn't exactly what Charles had told Heather. "Didn't Heather say that I was going to have everyone together for a dinner party in a couple of months?"

"Yes, but that is a dinner party. It's not a casual meeting in the middle of the day. Everything will be fine. We won't stay long."

"You didn't tell my parents that you helped me get better acquainted with Eris, did you?"

"Of course not! I only told them that I happened to meet her by accident the day I got lost on my way to the market and that you happened to be down there waiting for me. I stuck to our story."

"Thank you." The last thing he needed was for anyone to find out he had used Reina to end up marrying Eris. There were bound to be all kinds of questions, and he'd rather not answer them.

"I have a good memory, and I don't reveal secrets," Reina said. "You can trust me."

"I appreciate that."

The footman opened the front door, and Charles' mother ran over to hug him while his father took a more leisurely time to reach them.

"When we found out you ran off to elope, we worried something bad might happen while you were gone," his mother said as she let him go. She put her hand over her heart. "Thank goodness you're all right." She patted his cheeks. "One can't be too careful. Even if you are a gentleman, terrible things can still happen while you're traveling. Thieves are out there, you know."

"I know how to be careful," Charles replied. "Did you really worry that I would get robbed?"

"Only until Heather assured us you were fine," Charles' father spoke up. "It was a short time."

"It seemed like a long time to me," his mother replied. "My heart nearly stopped."

"It took two glasses of sherry every day to settle her nerves," Reina added.

"Well, I'm just glad my little boy is all right," his mother said and scanned the area. "Where is the lady you married?"

"Upstairs at the moment." Charles waved for them to go with him to the drawing room, and as they followed, he continued, "She's taking a bath."

"I knew we should have requested a visit," his father said.

"We're here now," Reina replied. "We might as well make the best of it."

After his family removed their coats and gloves, Charles instructed the butler to bring in tea and crumpets. He joined them and sat on the settee across from them.

"I admit that I was happy to hear the news," his father said. "I was beginning to worry you'd never marry. Then you'd never have a son, and I'd have no grandson to pass my title to."

"Yes, your father did worry about the future of his title," his mother agreed as she shifted into a comfortable position in the chair. "You've only been a suitor a couple of times, and those ladies ended up marrying someone else."

"I've been busy," Charles said. "A gentleman's wealth doesn't accumulate all by itself. It needs time."

"So does getting an heir," his mother insisted with a pointed look. "We're delighted Heather is giving us grandchildren, but we have a duty to the crown to pass on the title, and she's unable to do that."

"Which is why we're glad you finally married," his father added. "Although we were a bit disturbed you picked a widow still in mourning. And your friend's widow at that."

Yes, this was one of the reasons why Charles hadn't wanted them to know so soon. He knew the title and his choice in a bride would be two things that they'd mention.

"It's romantic," Reina said, saving him from having to find a suitable response. "Eris had hoped for a love match with Jonathan, but he suffered that terrible heart failure before she could get to know him all that well. Then Charles happened to see her and fell in love with her. The two are a perfect match. I think it's wonderful that two lonely people found each other."

Two lonely people? Charles frowned. Was his cousin really insisting he'd been lonely? He most certainly hadn't been. He'd been plenty busy. He'd barely had time to attend one of his parents' or Heather's dinner parties.

While courting Eris, he'd had to delay quite a few meetings with gentlemen of notable influence. Such a thing hadn't been easy to do, but it'd been necessary. For Jonathan's sake, he had upended his entire life.

"It would have been prudent to let Eris fulfill her period of mourning," Charles' father said. "Though, I recall meeting her, and she's not as young as most ladies. I suppose it was probably best not to wait. Her childbearing years are going to end soon."

"Love doesn't go by age," Reina replied. "Eris has plenty of time to have a child. She isn't that old. And what can anyone do about it now? Charles has already married her. Nine months from now, there might be an heir."

"But will that child be yours or Jonathan's?" Charles' father asked, directing his attention to Charles. "There's a reason ladies are expected to wait a year before marrying again."

Charles couldn't believe he had to address this, but he should have expected it. "Eris hadn't been with Jonathan that way. He died before anything happened."

"You're certain of that?" his father pressed.

"Yes," Charles replied. "I was with her. I saw the evidence of her innocence for myself."

"What evidence is that?" Reina asked.

"You don't need to know," Charles' father told her. "The important thing is that we'll be assured the child is the heir in our family line. Though, ideally, I suppose it's best if a little one doesn't come too soon or else people will wonder."

His mother nodded. "Yes. There needs to be at least a month to spare so the whispers won't taint the title."

"Charles married her a month after Jonathan died," Reina pointed out.

"That's true," his mother replied. "So long as he waited until they were married before doing anything, we should be fine."

Good grief. "I didn't do anything until we were married," Charles reluctantly assured them.

His mother seemed pleased with the news. "In that case, make sure you're diligent about the heir. The sooner you have a son, the sooner your poor father can be at ease."

"It's not easy to wait for your son to have an heir," his father agreed. "You might find that out someday if your son puts off marriage the same way you did."

The butler came in, and Charles was overwhelmed with relief. Glad for the distraction, Charles hurried to pour tea into everyone's cups, including the one Eris would drink from when she came down. This wasn't ideal. He would have preferred it if his parents had waited until the dinner party to meet Eris, but he supposed they were impatient to meet her. Now he knew where Heather got her impulsiveness from.

"What will you do with your townhouse?" his father asked after the butler left.

"I'll sell it eventually," Charles lied.

"It's unusual that a gentleman moves into his wife's townhouse," his mother said. "I can't think of any other gentleman who does it."

"I'm sure there have been a couple who have," Charles replied then took a bite of his crumpet so he was spared having to talk for a brief time.

"I think Charles is right," Reina said, a thoughtful tone in her voice. "If I remember correctly, Mr. Jasper moved into his wife's townhouse when he married her. Mr. Jasper is Heather's husband's friend's brother-in-law."

Charles' eyes nearly popped out of his head as he struggled to process exactly what she'd just said. He was acquainted with Mr. Jasper since Mr. Jasper excelled at investing, but he didn't know him well enough to know the people he was related to. Heather's husband was Gill, and he knew for a fact that Mr. Jasper and Gill were not friends.

Come to think of it, he was barely aware of who Gill associated with. While he and Gill were now related, he didn't have much to do with him beyond the times the family all got together. Gill seemed more interested in leisurely pursuits and spent his free time with gentlemen who preferred the same. Charles never had use for intended idleness. All things considered, however, he was glad Gill treated his sister well and was a good father to his nephew. So really, all was well.

"I know someone who would like to buy a townhouse," Charles' father said. "He'll give you a good price for yours."

Charles finished his crumpet and cleared his throat. "I'm in no hurry to sell it. I plan to wait."

"How long are you going to wait?" his mother asked.

Charles shrugged. "I don't know. I hadn't thought that far."

"I see no reason why you should wait when you're married and living here," his mother replied. "It makes no sense."

"Everything happened so suddenly," Charles said. "I'm waiting for things to go back to normal."

"Everything is happening suddenly because you wanted to rush into marriage," his mother pointed out. "Why didn't you take time to let Eris go through the mourning period if you wished to take things slow?"

Reina chuckled. "He was in love. You can't expect someone so completely in love to wait. It'd be cruel."

"It also seems cruel to delay selling a perfectly good townhouse that isn't being lived in," his mother said.

"I agree with your aunt," Charles' father told Reina. "The person I know could use a townhouse right away. He could pay for the townhouse today if Charles would just agree to sell it."

Charles silently cursed Heather for telling his parents that he had returned to London. This was all her fault. Since she couldn't wait, he was being put into a very uncomfortable spot. He could not, under any circumstance, let them know the truth until he had the proof he needed. If he rushed to tell them without proof, they'd accuse him of being foolish like they had the time when he tracked Heather down after Heather eloped.

Reina jumped to her feet and ran to the doorway so she could hug Eris who had just entered the room. "We couldn't wait to welcome you to the family," Reina told her. "Tell us how Charles convinced you to run off with him to Gretna Green. I want to hear every detail!"

Charles set the cup on the table and went over to them before his cousin could overwhelm Eris. "There's plenty of time to go into all of that," he quietly told Reina so his parents didn't overhear. The less they knew, the better. "You should wait until you and Eris are alone. We don't have to do it while my parents are here."

"Oh, you're right," Reina said. "They'd rather get better acquainted with Eris anyway." Without waiting for Charles to take Eris' arm, she grabbed Eris' hand and took her to the settee. "You can sit with your husband."

Charles released his breath and returned to his spot on the settee. "I had no idea my family would be so anxious to meet you," he told Eris as he offered her some tea.

As Eris accepted it, Charles' father asked, "How are you doing, my dear?"

"I'm fine," Eris replied. "I hope no one is upset that Charles and I married so soon after Jonathan's death.

I know I haven't been through the proper length of mourning."

"All things considered, marrying as fast as you did is understandable," his father said.

Charles held his breath. His father wasn't going to start asking her about her ability to have children right away, was he?

"We are sorry, of course, that your marriage with Jonathan came to a swift and tragic end," his father continued. "Some things are out of our control, and the time of one's death is one of them. This marriage might be what you both need. You two were close to Jonathan. I'm sure it gives you comfort to be together."

Charles' mother smiled in approval. "That's well said. Sometimes grief can bring two people together."

"It was more than grief," Reina interrupted. "It was love. And I, for one, think love is worth pursuing regardless of what else is going on."

Charles' mother chuckled. "You are quite the romantic, Reina. In some ways, you remind me of Heather. But maybe there's a bit of Charles there, too." She turned her gaze to Charles and added, "I would never have thought you capable of eloping. I was sure you were going to wait for a long courtship then have the banns read. Ever since you were a child, you took your time with everything. You liked to have everything planned out so there were no surprises."

"That's all well and good until one falls in love," Reina insisted. "Why wait to marry someone if you know they are the one you want to share the rest of your life with?"

"I hope you don't elope, too," Charles' father told her. "I'd like to have at least one family member who will get married the proper way."

"We're not saying we disapprove of your marriage," Charles' mother hurried to tell Eris. "We heartily approve. We're glad Charles finally found a wife. We have a title in the family that will need to be passed down the line."

"That's enough, Mother," Charles said. "We don't need to go into all of that. I thought you wanted to learn about Eris."

"Yes, we do." His mother paused. "We weren't here for the wedding, but we did come here for the funeral. Of course, there were so many people that it was impossible to talk to everyone. Why is it we are more likely to gather everyone together for a funeral but not a wedding?"

His father's eyebrows furrowed. "I suppose it's because we know we'll never see the person again."

"But we're burying them," his mother replied. "They don't know who is there and who isn't."

"That's true. Perhaps funerals are more for the living than the dead," his father said. "I think people need others more when they're grieving. When you're celebrating, you're stronger in the heart."

Charles didn't want this conversation going in this direction. He and Eris were already wearing their mourning clothes, and he was here on behalf of his friend. His parents and Reina wore a black armband to show their condolences. He didn't feel like going down the morbid path of death. But he couldn't very well ignore what his parents were saying, either.

Inspired, Charles said, "Now you can see why Eris and I chose to go to Gretna Green. We both decided it was best to quietly marry, given the circumstances."

His parents glanced at each other again, and after a moment, they gave a nod of agreement.

"A wise decision," his mother said. "Once a person overcomes their shock, it makes the most sense. We don't need to draw any more attention to the marriage than necessary."

"You won't go to any balls or other social engagements any time soon, will you?" his father asked.

"No," Charles and Eris said at the same time.

"At least they're in agreement on that," his father told his mother. "That will make the Ton quiet down much sooner with the gossip."

"I did worry about what people would say," Eris said.

"She barely knew Jonathan," Reina inserted for her. "The marriage was arranged. It wasn't like they loved each other. I don't see why two people in love should have to wait an entire year before getting married."

"We're well aware of how you feel, Reina," Charles' father said. "You've made yourself very clear several times."

"I don't blame people for not agreeing with what we did," Eris spoke up after a long moment of silence. "I know how bad things appear. People will assume I didn't care anything about Jonathan. That's not true. I liked him. He seemed like a good person. He was kind and gentle, much like Charles is. It's just that I didn't get to know him long enough for anything more than a casual fondness to develop."

Charles stared at her. The tone of her voice and expression in her face indicated sincerity. There was nothing there that would lead anyone to think she was even capable of hurting his friend. It really did seem as if she had truly meant to be a good and faithful wife to Jonathan.

Charles blinked the thoughts away. What was wrong with him? He knew better. Jonathan *had* been murdered. He hadn't died because his heart suddenly decided to stop working. Something about his death was wrong. He knew it. Deep down, he was certain of this very fact.

So how could he reconcile that with how he'd just felt when Eris had talked about his friend just now?

"Sometimes God offers us a second chance," Charles' mother said, bringing him out of his thoughts. "No one can know the future. We have to make the best of our situation."

"Have you and Charles thought of any children's names?" Charles' father asked Eris.

Charles couldn't believe it. Did his father really have to ask something so personal?

Eris blushed but answered, "No, we haven't yet. I'm sure we will."

"Make sure you do," his father said. "Charles has been reluctant in giving proper thought to the future. He seems to think he has all the time in the world to have a child. Coming up with a few names before you need them shows proper diligence."

"There's no need to say anything else, Father," Charles told him. "Things like names can wait until there's a child on the way. Now," he hurried to add before they could continue on with this topic, "I thought you wanted to find out more about Eris."

"Yes," his mother said. "Tell us about yourself Eris. What interests do you have? What was life like for you while growing up? Who's in your family?"

While he was sure that was a lot of questions for Eris to absorb all at once, Charles didn't mind. His mother would remember the questions and keep asking them. She'd done the same with Gill after he married Heather. By the time the poor man was done, Charles knew way more about him than he thought was reasonable.

Charles picked up another crumpet and took a bite. If his mother made Eris uncomfortable, he would find a way to stop the questions.

He caught the enthusiastic smile on Reina's face and thought his cousin was more excited about the marriage than even Eris was. That could possibly be bad.

If Eris was guilty of murder, he couldn't let her get away with it. He had a duty to expose her. But if Eris was innocent, if it turned out he'd been wrong…

Then what?

Then he'd have to find out who really did it.

Chapter Sixteen

"You'll keep Eris out for at least an hour, won't you?" Charles asked early the next afternoon when he had invited Reina over so she would take Eris to the market.

Reina laughed as she adjusted her gloves. "I already told you I would." She glanced past him, and he looked over his shoulder to make sure Eris hadn't entered the drawing room yet.

Good. She hadn't.

Charles turned back to his cousin. "This evening's dinner party is important. I want to make sure everything goes well."

"Oh, how sweet. You love her so much. Why don't you come along? It would be nice to talk to you without your parents around to take up most of the conversation."

Charles shook his head. "I can't. I have something to do. But you two will have a good afternoon. I gave you plenty of money to pick up some candy or whatever it is you ladies like to do when you're out."

"Last week Eris did mention a shop that has the best chocolate. I'll have her take me there." She glanced around him, let out an excited cheer, and ran around him.

He turned in time to see Reina give Eris a hug.

"I can't tell you how relieved I am that you're still willing to be my friend after all the questions my aunt asked you," Reina told her.

"She had a right to be curious," Eris said. "I'm sure the elopement came as a shock to everyone. I didn't even meet her before marrying Charles."

"That wasn't your fault," Charles replied. "I was the one who wanted to rush things."

"Only because you were hopelessly in love and couldn't help yourself," Reina said. "I think it's so romantic. I hope when love comes for me, it'll be that way."

Charles hid his alarm. Had he unwittingly become a bad influence? It wasn't good if she was going to run off with the first gentleman who paid attention to her. "You need to make sure you know the gentleman before you marry him. What Eris and I did wasn't all that spontaneous. We both knew Jonathan."

"So?" Reina asked.

"So Jonathan wouldn't have agreed to marry Eris if she wasn't a suitable match." All night he'd been plagued with the idea that he had been wrong about Eris. Was it possible he had jumped to conclusions when he came up with the plan to marry her? Had someone else murdered Jonathan?

This was a very frustrating situation. He didn't know what to think, but he had to search Eris' bedchamber to get an idea of what the truth might be. The rest of the townhouse offered no clues. Surely, if she had murdered Jonathan, there would be something in her bedchamber to reveal the truth to him. A murderer couldn't be so skilled at the crime that they left no clues behind.

"I hope you two have a good afternoon while you're out," he told Eris and Reina. He gave Eris a quick kiss. "You don't have to rush home. Enjoy your time with my cousin."

"Yes, you can show me that chocolate shop," Reina said. "I love chocolate. candy"

"This shop has candy imported from other countries," Eris replied. "If you think you love chocolate candy now, just wait until you have the ones from France."

"I can't wait!"

The two headed out the front door, but Charles waited until they went to the carriage before he hurried up the stairs.

When he got to Eris' bedchamber, he shut the door so the servants wouldn't notice him. He didn't think any of the maids were doing laundry today, but just in case, he needed to be careful. There was no point in Eris finding out he had been snooping around her things.

He decided the most logical place a person would hide something was in a drawer, so he went straight to her dresser and sorted through everything he could find. He was mindful to keep everything in its proper place when he was done. His face did warm when he went through her undergarments, and he had to push aside the surge of pleasure that coursed through him at the reminder of being in bed with her. He'd been able to resist going to her bed last night since his desire to be with her had been satisfied the other night, but he might have to come in here tonight after sorting through her intimate items.

He wished he wasn't so weak. He had no idea that being with a lady could be so addicting. No wonder gentlemen ended up becoming rakes if they didn't marry.

Forcing the thought aside, he left the dresser and went to the vanity. He stopped when he saw a small gold music box. It was next to the assortment of combs, brushes, and hairpins. The object was small enough to hold in the palm of his hand. It was tucked along the corner of the vanity. It was out of the way of the things Eris needed to get ready for each day, but it was also in a place where she could see it every time she sat here.

He picked it up. It looked familiar. He was sure he'd seen this before. He played the music, and at once a memory came to him.

He and Jonathan had been walking through the market when Jonathan got the inclination to enter a shop selling trinkets. Jonathan found a music box and had asked Charles what he thought of the music.

"Do you think this is something a lady would like?" Jonathan had asked him.

Charles had shrugged and said, "Who can understand what ladies like? We can bring Heather here or even Reina if you want a lady's opinion."

Jonathan had declined the offer but went through a few music boxes before paying for this one. At the time, Charles had thought Jonathan wished to give a cousin or an aunt this gift. He hadn't thought Jonathan had bought it for Eris.

And Eris still had it. She hadn't gotten rid of it. She had it out where she could see it every day.

He doubted someone would keep a gift from someone she murdered. It would be a reminder of her crime. More than that, why would she want to keep a gift from someone she killed? It didn't make sense.

Why hadn't he noticed this music box when he had been in here the other night?

What a ridiculous question. At the time, he hadn't been preoccupied with thoughts of his friend's death. He'd been caught up in satisfying his body's base desires. It really was alarming how demanding the human body could be. And what gentleman would expect something of importance to be right in the open on a lady's vanity?

Charles placed the music box in its spot, careful to make sure it was exactly where it was before.

He wasn't sure what to make of this new information. He hadn't expected to find something that proved Eris had planned to spend the rest of her life with Jonathan when she married him.

And this proof matched the tone of her voice when she had spoken about Jonathan yesterday when his parents and Reina were here. While she talked, he'd been convinced that she had cared for Jonathan.

But Jonathan was murdered. I know it. Something about his death just doesn't make sense. If Eris didn't kill him, then who did?

Before he could remove her as a suspect, he had to search the rest of the room. He'd never find any peace if he didn't. He had to follow every logical path he could find.

He searched the drawers of the vanity. Then he looked through the armoire and the desk in the small room off to the side of the bedchamber. He searched every place a person might hide something, but there was nothing that pointed to her being the killer.

He didn't know where to go from here. There was no one else he knew who might have wanted Jonathan dead. Except possibly Eris' brother.

Was it possible Byron had arranged the marriage so he could kill Jonathan? Maybe he had snuck in here on the wedding night and slipped into Jonathan's bedchamber. He was a Runner. Runners knew how to do things like get into places they shouldn't be. They were considered exceptionally skilled in solving crimes. Someone who knew how to solve a crime would probably be good at committing one.

Yes, it had to be the brother. It was strange that Eris' brother had shown up right after he and Eris had come back from Gretna Green, wasn't it? He was here before the *Tittletattle* had time to post his return with Eris. Even Heather hadn't been here that quickly, and she belonged to a lady's group who made it a point to know the latest gossip.

Charles frowned. Runners didn't make a lot of money. He recalled the snide comment Byron had made about not having the kind of time to waste like wealthy gentlemen did, as if he thought all Charles had to do was sit around while money magically came his way.

Was it possible that when Byron found out how wealthy Jonathan was, he had arranged the marriage between Eris and Jonathan for the sole purpose of allowing his sister to inherit the money? Then he could rely on her to give him money whenever he wanted it?

Charles frowned. Eris did seem unusually trusting. Look at how quickly she believed he was sincere about falling in love with her. She hadn't even questioned it. She'd even naively went with him to Gretna Green without telling anyone about it. Charles could have done anything to her along the way. She didn't know he was an honorable gentleman who would never dream of hurting a lady.

Yes, she was much too trusting. Her brother had to know that. Her brother probably used her. She had been a spinster. She'd had no prospects for marriage. Jonathan was so good-hearted and kind that her brother could have talked him into the arranged marriage. Also, Jonathan needed an heir. Despite Eris' age, she was an attractive prospect for marriage. She wasn't like those silly-minded young ladies who were prone to gossiping and giggling all the time. She was a sensible lady who could hold a conversation. It was no wonder Jonathan had agreed to the union.

The more Charles thought it over, the more certain he was that Byron was the murderer. Byron had planned everything out. He had arranged the marriage and pretended to be happy about the union. Then, while Jonathan was getting ready in his bedchamber to consummate the marriage, Byron had snuck into the house and killed him.

As a Runner, Byron knew how to be quiet. Eris wouldn't have heard a thing. Being a virgin, she would have been too shy to check on Jonathan. So when he came into the townhouse to kill Jonathan, she had stayed in her bed all night. Then, in the morning, a servant happened to find Jonathan's body, and that's when Eris found out he was dead.

It all made sense! That was how it all happened. Now that the pieces were falling into place, it was easy to see the truth.

Her brother was coming over this evening for a dinner party. Good. Charles would have the perfect opportunity to speak with him. He wasn't exactly sure what he would talk to Byron about in order to get to the truth, but he was going to come up with something. With his new mission in mind, he went to his bedchamber to plan out the evening.

Chapter Seventeen

"Is something troubling you?" Eris asked that evening as Charles stood at the window in the drawing room.

His gaze swept the street. No sign of a carriage or a lone gentleman walking in the direction of this townhouse. He forced his attention to her and smiled at how lovely she looked. Her hair had been pulled back into an attractive style, and she wore a black gown to honor Jonathan. It was nice to know she was sincere about caring for his friend. Jonathan should not be forgotten.

Nor should his death go unavenged. His gaze returned to the window. Still nothing.

Eris walked over to him. "Charles?"

He forced his attention back to her.

"If you're nervous about this evening, you don't need to be," she said. "My brother will like you. You're a wonderful gentleman."

It was sweet that she worried about him. He slipped his arm around her waist and drew her closer to him. "It doesn't matter what your brother thinks of me. All that matters is what you think."

She was bound to be disappointed when she realized her brother was a cold-blooded killer. Thankfully, he would be here to help her through it. He'd hate to think of what would happen if she had to go through that kind of pain alone.

He kissed her. "You have a tender heart, my love. I did well when I married you."

She smiled and got ready to reply when Charles saw his parents' carriage.

"Reina's here," he said and gave her another kiss before he hurried to the front door.

He ought to warn his cousin about Byron. He wouldn't come out and tell her what he suspected about him, but she couldn't entertain the possibility that he could be her suitor.

"I'll get it," he told the footman.

The footman's eyebrows rose in surprise, but he stepped away from the door and let Charles open it. Charles met his cousin just as she made it halfway up the steps.

Reina laughed. "I can't recall a time I've seen you so excited. This is going to be a fun dinner party."

Ignoring her comment, he said, "I have something important to tell you, but it's something you must keep secret. You can't even bring it up this evening."

Her eyebrows furrowed. "Don't tell me you ran off to elope because you thought you might have gotten Eris with child."

His eyes grew wide. "No. It's nothing like that." He was shocked she would even think such a thing. Had all the times he'd told her to be mindful of her virtue been for nothing? "I only wanted to tell you that Eris' brother is secretly betrothed. He doesn't want anyone to know because he's a Runner. Gentlemen who are Runners don't like everyone to know what they're doing. The secrecy makes them feel important." Before she could argue the logic of his statement, he added, "The reason I'm telling you this is so that you don't develop any romantic feelings for him."

"Oh, I already fancy someone. You have nothing to worry about." She patted his arm then continued up the stairs.

"You do? Who?" he asked as he followed her.

"I'd rather not say. The feelings are too new, and I don't even know if he feels the same way. It'd be terribly embarrassing if I were to tell you and then find out he'd rather marry someone else."

"Marriage? You're thinking of marrying him?"

"Well, the thought did occur to me when I was talking to him."

"I don't like the sound of this." Especially since it was happening much too fast. "Do I even know this gentleman?"

They reached the entryway, and she turned to face him. "I've barely spent any time with him. That's why I need to wait for an opportune moment so I can talk to him. I need to figure out if he shares my feelings or not. Until then, I want to keep his identity to myself. Now, regarding Eris' brother, I'll keep what you told me in confidence. In return, you will respect my right to keep my secret to myself."

He stared at her for a moment then sighed. "In some ways, you're too much like my sister. I hope you show better sense than she did. Don't kidnap the poor gentleman in order to marry him."

"I have no desire to do something so silly."

They reached the front door, and they saw that Eris was waiting for them a few feet away.

Reina hurried over to her. "You are so beautiful! It's no wonder my cousin had to run off and marry you as quickly as he did."

Charles got ready to shut the door when someone said, "It's not polite to slam a door in your guest's face."

Charles jerked and peered around the door. It was Byron. "How is it possible I didn't notice you coming up the steps?" Charles asked.

Byron shrugged. "How would I know? You're the only one who can answer that question. Quite frankly, I'm shocked you didn't notice me."

Charles bit his tongue so he wouldn't say anything to raise the gentleman's suspicions. Byron had to be the killer. Look at how quietly he had come up the stairs.

Neither Charles nor Reina had noticed him. Come to think of it, Charles hadn't even spotted him on the street. That was one form of evidence. Byron could sneak into Jonathan's bedchamber without anyone, even poor Jonathan, being the wiser. Charles was going to have to be diligent around him.

Byron went over to Eris and hugged her. "I hope you're doing well."

"I am," Eris replied. "This is Reina. She's become a very good friend in a short amount of time. Reina, this is Byron, my brother."

Byron bowed. "It's a pleasure to make your acquaintance."

As Reina returned the greeting, Charles turned to close the door, making sure no one else was coming up the steps of the townhouse. While no one else had been invited, he didn't need to be caught missing someone else. Since no one was on the stairs, he shut the door and went to the others.

"We went out this afternoon and bought some of those graphite pencils you like," Eris told Byron. "The gentleman who made them sanded the wood so they'll be easy to hold."

"We're going to have so much fun drawing silhouettes," Reina added. "You two gentlemen have such noble profiles."

Charles frowned. He didn't like that she had included Byron in that compliment. Byron might think she was flirting with him and try to charm her. While

Reina claimed to have an interest in someone else, that could easily change at any time. He hoped his lie about Byron being betrothed was enough.

"We should go into the drawing room," Eris said. "We'll be more comfortable if we're sitting."

Charles followed the others into the room, and when Eris gave him a cup of tea, he took it. He was supposed to sit with Eris, but he decided to sit in the chair next to Reina in order to further do his part to make sure his cousin didn't fall in love with Byron.

Byron's eyebrows rose. "Don't you want to sit with your wife?"

"You're Eris' brother. I thought you might want to sit with her," Charles said.

"Considering she's your wife, that's unusual," Byron replied.

"I don't mind, Byron," Eris said. "Here. Have some tea." She held a cup out to him.

Byron glanced at Charles in a way that told Charles he didn't like him then sat next to her on the settee.

Charles bit his tongue and settled back in his chair. He didn't care for Byron, either, but he was determined not to give that away. It would only make the gentleman wonder if Charles had figured out the truth about Jonathan's death. Charles crossed his legs and took a sip of the tea.

"I put the things for drawing silhouettes over there on the table," Eris said, gesturing to the table by the window in the corner of the room. "I even have the candles ready."

"It's going to be fun," Reina replied. "You did a wonderful job of setting everything up."

Eris offered her a grateful smile and then drank her tea.

A few tense moments passed in silence. Charles tried to watch Byron without staring at him outright. Byron, however, didn't seem inclined to hide his interest in Charles since whenever Charles peeked in his direction, Byron was looking directly at him.

"Eris and I had so much fun shopping this afternoon," Reina finally spoke up. "We came across the funniest couple. They were obviously in love, but they bickered the whole time we were in the candy shop."

Eris chuckled. "They were funny. I've seen them before at a couple of balls. It was Mr. Robinson and his wife, if I recall correctly. They always act like that. I think they enjoy the silly arguments. Nothing they ever say is serious. You can tell they are only teasing each other."

"It sounds like a fun marriage." Reina glanced between Charles and Byron. "I suppose since this is a private dinner party, it's all right to say that I actually saw Mr. Robinson give her a playful pat on the bottom when he didn't think anyone was looking." She giggled.

Surprised his cousin should find this amusing, Charles said, "I fail to understand why he would do something so inappropriate in public." Exchanging witty banter was one thing, but him touching her somewhere private like that wasn't the least bit acceptable. "I hope you understand you shouldn't allow your future husband to do anything like that."

"He didn't realize I saw it. He made an effort to be discreet."

"Well, he wasn't discreet if you noticed," Charles pointed out then drank more tea.

"She was quick to reprimand him," Reina said.

"At least she had the sense to do that. I hope he listens so that he doesn't do that again," Charles replied.

Reina gave a slight roll of her eyes. "In all the time I've been in London, it doesn't seem like people have much fun."

"They have fun. They just know that it's best to have fun in the privacy of their homes."

"There's a lot that can happen in the privacy of one's home," Byron said.

Charles tensed. He sensed there was a subtle meaning Byron had just slipped into those words. Giving up the pretense of not looking at him, Charles made direct eye contact with him. "What did you mean by that?"

"Nothing. I was merely agreeing with you," Byron replied.

Charles frowned. Was he, or was he lying?

"I don't see the harm in an affectionate pat while out in public," Reina said. "Perhaps it might have been better if he'd touched her arm or the small of her back, but it was still a sweet gesture."

"Some gentlemen like to be scandalous, but they also don't want to get found out," Eris replied. "They find it exciting to try to do something the Ton wouldn't like without getting caught. Gossip spreads quickly, and it's hard to restore your reputation once you lose it, especially if you're a lady. My advice, Reina, is that it's best not to do anything in public that could potentially lead to a scandal."

"That was well said," Charles agreed, pleased Eris could see the wisdom in being diligent with one's reputation. Eris would be a good influence on his cousin. It was good they were friends.

"No one but me noticed," Reina said. "I'd say he was careful."

Something akin to respect came across Byron's face. "It's not everyone who notices everything that happens around them."

Charles' attention went back to him. He didn't need for Byron to find something attractive in his cousin. He had to put a stop to this before it got serious. He cleared his throat and straightened up in the chair. "I hope everyone likes venison. Cook assured me it's fresh. He said the maid picked it up from the market this afternoon."

"It's a shame your father isn't here," Reina said. "He loves venison." Glancing at the others, she added, "He'd eat it for every meal if he could."

"Why didn't you invite the rest of your family over?" Byron asked Charles. "It would have been nice to meet them."

Charles detected a challenge in the gentleman's comment, as if he thought Charles might be doing something deceptive, which was absurd given that Charles hadn't been the one who killed Jonathan. "I wanted this to be a small gathering since it's the first dinner party Eris and I are hosting," Charles said after a moment.

"Just how many parents do you have?" Byron asked.

Charles didn't know what to make of the ridiculous question, but he answered, "Two, just like everyone else."

"So what would have been the difference between four and six people?" Byron asked.

"What is this about, Byron?" Eris interrupted.

"If the purpose was to bring our families together, then why only pick a cousin?" Byron replied. "Think of it, Eris. You and I are all that's left. Our parents are no longer alive, and we have no close relatives. Your new husband, however, has quite a few close relatives. He has two living parents, three sisters, and this cousin. The oldest sister is married with a child and another on the way. Why didn't he invite everyone?"

Charles stiffened. "How do you know all of that? And how did you know my oldest sister is with child?" Heather had only told the family about it. She'd wanted to wait until she was further along in her pregnancy before announcing it to everyone in London.

"I'm a Runner," Byron told him. "And an experienced one."

Charles didn't like the sound of this. Had Byron been investigating his family?

Eris laughed. "You shouldn't try to frighten him, Byron." She glanced at Charles. "I probably mentioned everyone when he stopped by the other day."

"Do you remember telling him all of that?" Charles asked her.

She paused then replied, "No, but I probably said something in passing at some point while I told him about our elopement. Everything's happened so fast over the past few weeks. I can hardly remember everything I said."

"A whirlwind romance will do that to a person," Reina said.

Ignoring Reina, Byron looked at Eris. "Have you met Charles' parents or other family members yet?"

"I've met the parents and oldest sister," Eris said.

"And how long were they here?" Byron asked.

"Oh, I don't know. We had tea, and that was pretty much it," Eris replied.

"I was there when Charles' parents were here," Reina told Byron. "We didn't want to disturb Charles and Eris since they're still newly married. We weren't here for longer than an hour."

Byron glanced at Charles. "If she's already met some of your family, why not let me meet them, too?"

"What's the point? It seems like you know plenty about them already," Charles replied, struggling to keep his tone pleasant for the sake of the two ladies who were watching them.

"Something is strange about all of this," Byron said, turning his gaze back to Eris. "If this was truly a dinner party where the families are to meet, then the parents, at least, should be here."

Charles bristled. How dare he! Byron was trying to convince his innocent and naïve sister that she shouldn't trust her husband. Charles didn't like this. He didn't like it one bit. He had nothing to hide. He wasn't the murderer in this room!

"I don't like where this is going," Charles told him.

"If that's the case, you shouldn't have gotten involved with my sister," Byron said.

Charles' eyes grew wide. Was that a threat? Was Byron planning to kill him in order to get him out of the way so that no one would find out he had killed Jonathan?

Reina's eyebrows furrowed, and Eris seemed equally confused.

"I want this evening to go well," Eris finally said after a tense moment. "This is the first time I've been able to have a dinner party in my house. Can't we have a pleasant evening?"

"It's a shame you didn't have time to host a dinner party with Jonathan," Byron told her, though he didn't take his gaze off of Charles.

Eris' smile faltered. "I don't think anything could have been done about that, Byron. It was tragic that Jonathan died."

"Yes, it was," Charles agreed, keeping his attention focused on Byron. "My good friend of many years was gone well before his time."

The room fell into an uneasy silence, and a minute later the butler came to announce that dinner was ready.

If it was up to Charles, he'd take Byron to the front door and kick him out. Byron was the murderer. There was no doubt about it. And now he was going to get rid of him, too. Charles stood in Byron's way of the money Jonathan left Eris. Byron needed him out of the way in order to get to it. And not only would Byron get to Jonathan's money, he would get to the significant sum of money Charles had as well. Charles couldn't believe he had been so blind on the day of Jonathan's funeral. He should have seen how wicked Eris' brother was sooner.

"Since dinner is ready, we should eat," Reina said, glancing between Charles and Byron. "I don't know about everyone else, but I sure am hungry. Venison sounds delicious."

"Yes, it does," Eris hurried to add. "Charles had Cook prepare a wonderful meal. He even asked for lemon cheesecakes. You love those, Byron."

Did he? If Charles had known that, he wouldn't have asked for them to be put on the menu.

Reina stood up. "Well, come on, then. Let's get up. The dinner won't come to us."

While it wasn't ideal, Charles was going to have to go through the rest of the evening with Byron in his home. He was going to have to endure this most unwelcome guest until it was time for everyone to retire for the night.

Charles rose to his feet and extended his arm to Eris. "We'll go after you and Reina," he told Byron.

Eris stood up from the settee and went over to take Charles' arm. She glanced at Byron.

After making eye contact with his sister, Byron finally offered his arm to Reina.

Charles waited until Byron and Reina were in front of him before escorting Eris out of the room. He put his hand over Eris' and offered her a comforting smile. The poor lady. He was going to have to spend a lot of time consoling her once her brother's crime was exposed. If it was the last thing he did, he was going to prove, beyond a reasonable doubt, that Byron was guilty. And he was going to do it before Byron got the chance to kill him.

Chapter Eighteen

The dinner party had been a disaster. Eris didn't know why, but it was apparent her brother didn't approve of Charles. After a very tense dinner, she had feigned a headache so that Byron and Reina had to leave early. She couldn't, in good conscience, continue to make Charles uncomfortable. She had to find out why Byron didn't like him, but she would need to do that at a time when they could be alone.

After Eris was ready for bed, she sat at the vanity. She didn't know if she could sleep without talking to Charles about how the evening went.

With a deep breath, she stood up from the vanity and went to the door separating her bedchamber with Charles'. Forcing aside her nervousness, she tapped on it. She pulled the robe closer around herself and waited for Charles to answer.

He opened the door, and to her surprise, he was still dressed.

She cleared her throat. "I wanted to apologize for what my brother did this evening. I don't know what possessed him to be so rude."

Charles took her by the arm and encouraged her to come into his bedchamber. "You have nothing to apologize for. I'm just sorry the evening turned out the way it did. I know you were looking forward to this evening. You and Reina even went out to buy those graphite pencils to draw silhouettes."

"I can draw silhouettes anytime. All I wanted was for everyone to have a pleasant evening. I'm disappointed in my brother. If I had known he was going to behave the way he did, I would have just said we should invite Reina or maybe even Algernon. The dinner party we had with them went so wonderfully."

"Yes, that was a good evening. We'll invite them both over in the future. We'll also have a dinner party with my entire family. I just hope my mother is done asking you so many questions."

She chuckled. "I didn't mind. I was relieved I didn't have to come up with something to say. I've never done well with larger groups. I end up sitting by myself and hope people will come over to talk to me. Byron knows that about me. I don't understand why he was upset more people weren't with us tonight."

Charles brought her into his arms and kissed her. "You have nothing to explain to me. Our marriage happened so suddenly. With that and Jonathan's death, we have enough to contend with."

Noting the slight pain in his voice at the mention of his friend, she whispered, "I'm glad to be married to you, but I do regret that you lost your friend."

He offered her a smile. "I know you do, and it's one of the things I appreciate most about you." He took her by the arm and led her further into the room. "I wish Jonathan had left more things behind. I didn't realize he kept so little to reflect his life."

"The only time I was in this room was when I found the cane for you. I didn't know what he held onto before then." She glanced around the room. It seemed that Charles had more personal belongings than Jonathan had.

"I'm glad you knocked on the door. I don't want to be alone tonight. Will you stay with me?"

Her face warmed, but she managed to murmur a shy, "Yes."

Given what happened this evening, she hadn't expected him to want to be in bed with her tonight. But she did enjoy being intimate with him and welcomed the chance to do so now.

He went to the dresser and began to remove his waistcoat. She hadn't watched him undress before, and doing so now, especially when she was just standing nearby, made her uncomfortable. Should she take off her robe? Should she go over to him? Should she go over to the bed? Should she stay where she was and wait for him to approach her?

"Would you rather we go to your bed?" Charles asked.

She turned her attention from the door that connected their bedchambers so she could look at him, and though they had been together before, she couldn't bring herself to look below his chest. "Would it be better if we were in there? I've never been in your bed to," she cleared her throat, "try for an heir."

He looked as if he was ready to say something but then settled for saying, "No. It's fine that we're in here."

She furrowed her eyebrows. Was there something she didn't know but should?

He set the last of his clothing on the dresser then went to the bed and pulled back the covers. Her heartbeat picked up as he approached her. He had the heated gaze in his eyes that let her know he was eager to be with her. And that heated gaze thrilled her to no end.

He cupped her face in his hands and kissed her. She leaned into him and returned his kiss, and after a moment, he wrapped his arms around her and drew her closer to him.

He continued kissing her, and before long, she felt her shyness giving way to the desire to be intimate with him. She didn't know if she'd ever get over the initial shyness that always came over her when she was with him this way, but she supposed it didn't matter. The point was that she was with him and they had a love match. Marriage was much better than she could have ever dreamed possible.

Charles traced the bottom of her lower lip with his tongue, and she parted her lips to let him into her mouth. He let out a low moan and released the strings of her robe. Her skin tingled in pleasure when he slipped his hands under her robe and began to explore her breasts.

She let out a contented sigh and wove her fingers through the hair at the nape of his neck. She loved his hair. It was soft to the touch. One of the things she secretly admired about him was how thick and shiny his hair was. She would like for her hair to be like this, but hers was thinner and not nearly as soft. She hoped if they had children, they would have his hair.

Charles' hands lowered to her abdomen, and the flesh between her legs ached in anticipation. He cupped her behind and lifted her off her feet. She instinctively put her legs around his waist and held onto him.

He settled her on the bed and kissed her for a while longer before he started to explore her in earnest with his hands. She couldn't be sure, but she thought he wasn't in such a hurry this time. He seemed to be taking more time kissing and touching her than he had the other two times they'd been together. She wondered if that was somehow significant.

He left a trail of kisses from her neck and worked his way down to her breasts. He took turns with each nipple, tracing one and lightly sucking on it before going to the other. Her nipples, as it turned out, were one of the most sensitive parts of her body, and as he continued his ministrations, it was getting harder and harder for her to keep track of the time.

She moaned and squeezed his shoulders in silent encouragement for him to continue with what he was doing. She'd never been aware of just how receptive her body was to touching and kissing before. Yes, she had gotten pleasure from the other two times, but this was much more intense. It felt as if she was hurling toward something she had no control over.

At some point, he brought his hand between her legs and traced the folds of her flesh. She spread her legs for him, and he slid two fingers into her. She let out a moan and shifted so that he was deeper into her. He stroked her core in earnest, and, on its own accord, her hips rocked with the rhythm of his thrusting.

She dug her fingers into his shoulders and urged him to keep doing this to her. The moment was so incredibly wonderful, so incredibly intense, that she was unable to concentrate on anything but the tension that was building up between her legs. And then, when she thought she couldn't possibly take it anymore, a burst of pleasure erupted within her. She cried out and tightened her hold on him. Waves of pleasure consumed her, and all she could do was remain still and let the waves come as they wished.

She had no idea how long it was until her body relaxed, but she did note the way Charles continued to caress her as he left a trail of kisses down her abdomen.

He lowered his head even further and continued exploring her in a way that continued to bring her much pleasure. A lady could get used to this kind of thing.

When he was satisfied with exploring her, he rose up and got between her legs. Though she'd been a bit shy to see him naked their other times together, she had snuck in a couple of peeks during their lovemaking, and she was surprised that there was nothing covering that part of him that was between his legs.

"Where is it?" she asked in surprise as he settled between her legs.

"Where is what?" he murmured as he kissed her neck.

"The thing you put down there," she replied, her curiosity getting the best of her despite the fact that his lips felt good against her skin.

"Thing?"

"It's like a stocking, except it can't be."

He stopped kissing her and brought his head up so he was looking directly at her. He seemed hesitant to respond, but after a moment, he said, "It's a sheath. I wasn't sure I wanted children right away, so I wore it. But now I know I want children. I don't plan to use it again."

She hadn't expected that kind of answer. She'd thought all gentlemen wanted children, especially those who had a title to pass on. She had assumed the covering had just been something all gentlemen wore during this act. For what purpose, she hadn't had the slightest idea.

Now, however, she knew, and it baffled her that he would want to delay trying for an heir, especially given her age.

He cupped the side of her face and gave her a lingering kiss. When he lifted his head back up, he said, "I love you, Eris. I'm ready to have children, and I want to have them with you."

He brought his mouth back to hers, letting her know he had no more to say on the subject, and she decided she didn't, either. Their marriage had been sudden. He just hadn't been ready yet for the possibility of children. But now he was, and she hoped she would get with child because she looked forward to having them.

He kissed her for a while before he entered her. She wrapped her legs around his waist and pulled him deeper into her. The sense of urgency he'd displayed the other two times came back, and he established the rhythm she was familiar with. It was a rhythm that let her know just how much he enjoyed doing this activity with her.

When he grew taut and stilled, she noticed that he was throbbing inside her. She tried to recall if she had picked up on that before, but she really had no idea. She did, however, note the fact that she was wetter than she'd been the other times when he pulled out of her. That had to be the difference, then, when a gentleman was trying to have an heir. So wearing a sheath prevented the part of him that could get her with child from going into her.

Charles settled next to her and started to bring her into his arms when she got tangled in the robe. She chuckled as he struggled to figure out a way to get it off of her.

"I should probably return to my room," she said. "It'd be pointless to remove it."

"Nonsense," he replied as he finally succeeded in removing it from her. He tossed the robe over to the dresser, but it fell to the floor. "I want you to be with me tonight."

"All through the night?"

He pulled the covers up to them and took her into his arms. "Yes, all through the night. I'd like to be with you in the morning when I wake up."

That was strange considering how he hadn't spent the entire night with her in bed before, but she reasoned that she wasn't the only one who was growing more comfortable in this marriage. He was, too. They were both getting used to the other. With a smile, she relaxed next to him and closed her eyes. In short time, she drifted off to sleep.

***

Ever since Charles could remember, he made it a habit of getting out of bed as soon as he woke up. The next morning, however, when he stirred from sleep, he decided to stay in bed and draw Eris closer to him.

This was nice. In the past, he hadn't bothered to think about what it might be like to wake up in bed with a lady. He'd been too busy with the pursuit of making money to care about ladies. This morning, however, he was given over to thoughts of how pleasant it was to have a lady in his life.

He wanted to spend the rest of his life with Eris. He wanted to have children with her, and, if they had a son, he'd like to name the child after Jonathan. He would need Eris' permission to do that, of course, but he had a feeling she would agree to it.

Perhaps they'd have more than one child. More than one might be nice. Regardless of whether they were boys or girls, he would teach them how to be wise with money. His sister might have a tendency to be impulsive, but she had heeded the words of their father and was diligent with the money given to her.

Then there would be the things he and Eris would do with their children. They could take them to the menagerie and circus. They would take walks through Hyde Park. They might even chance a hot air balloon ride. He'd always been intrigued by those but hadn't had a reason to go on one.

Then their children could spend time with his sister's children. Now that he was assured Eris wasn't the lady he had assumed her to be when he married her, he could allow Heather to be friends with her. And he wouldn't have to give Reina the unfortunate news that she'd have to end her friendship with Eris. All would be fine.

He didn't know how long he let his mind wander into all the things he anticipated about the future before

Eris woke up. He turned onto his side and greeted her with a kiss. The kiss turned into another one, and then it led to more until he realized there was no way he was going to be able to get through the day without satisfying his baser needs. Thankfully, Eris didn't seem to mind. In fact, she voiced her enjoyment for the activity, and knowing she was as excited about it as he was came as a great relief. He'd hate to think he was inconveniencing her by keeping her in bed longer than she was used to.

When they were done making love, he spent some time kissing and holding her before he finally convinced himself he needed to let the poor lady take a bath and get ready for the day. He was sure she had things she wanted to do. He couldn't expect her to spend all of her time with him.

He got out of the bed so he could give her the robe she'd been wearing the night before. Half of it was under the dresser. As he bent down to pull it out, something scraped across the floor. Surprised, he got on his knees and peered under the dresser. Closer to the wall, he saw something round and white. Eyebrows furrowed, he reached under the dresser to grab the small object. It was cool and smooth to the touch. He drew it out then searched the rest of the floor under the dresser. There was nothing else under it.

He sat up and inspected the object. It was a pearl button, and it had the design of a lion drawn into it. The lion was so detailed that Charles knew it had to be expensive.

Jonathan hadn't owned a button like this. Charles was sure he'd never seen anything like this on any of Jonathan's clothes, but he would check to make sure none of his clothes had anything like this on them.

If Jonathan didn't have any buttons like this, this button could very well be the proof he'd been looking for.

"What is that?" Eris asked.

Unaware she'd come up to him, Charles rose to his feet and helped her slip into her robe. Once she had the strings tied, he showed her the button. "Have you seen this before?"

She frowned as she studied it. "No, but it looks expensive."

Yes, it did look expensive. More expensive than something a Runner could afford.

And that thought bothered Charles more than he wanted to admit. What if Byron wasn't the killer? What if someone else had murdered Jonathan?

If Jonathan didn't have any similar buttons on his clothes, then this button had to belong to someone else. It would have been from someone who had snuck into this bedchamber and killed Jonathan. There would have been a struggle. Jonathan hadn't wanted to die. He'd had the rest of his life to live for. He had just gotten married. He was looking forward to having a family. So Jonathan would have fought the killer, and during the struggle, Jonathan must have pulled this button off of the gentleman's clothing. And, as a result, the button ended up rolling under the dresser.

He turned his attention back to Eris and gave her a kiss. “Why don’t you go on and get ready for the day? I’ll meet you in the drawing room in an hour for breakfast.”

“All right.” She smiled and headed to her room.

He waited until she shut the door before he went to search through Jonathan’s clothes which were still in the small room off to the side of the bedchamber.

Chapter Nineteen

The carriage came to a stop, and Eris braced herself for the unpleasant conversation she was about to have with her brother. She had to speak with him about last evening. She couldn't let this happen again. Charles was her husband, and he deserved to be treated with respect.

As she walked up to the middle-class home her brother rented, she worked through how she would begin their conversation. She had to find the perfect balance between being kind and being firm.

Before she reached the front door, her brother opened it. In the past, she had joked that he should be a footman since he had the uncanny ability to tell when someone was coming by to see him. All he'd said was that he was a Runner, and it was a Runner's duty to be aware of everything that was happening.

"I'm glad you came here," Byron said. "I wanted to talk to you without your husband around."

Her eyebrows furrowed. "You did?"

He nodded and waved for her to enter his home. "I was going to have a word with you at the dinner party after we ate, but I didn't get the chance since you ended up not feeling well."

"Yes, I want to talk to you about that." She passed him and waited for him to shut the door before adding, "I wasn't pleased with the way things went yesterday."

"Good. Then you're aware of the problem."

Surprised, her eyes grew wide. "Problem?"

"With Charles." He took her by the arm and led her to the sitting room.

"Yes, I figured you didn't like him."

He stopped her in front of the settee. "Have a seat, Eris. I'll get you something to drink."

"I'm not thirsty."

Despite her protest, he went to the pitcher on a nearby table and poured water into two glasses.

With a sigh, she got as comfortable as she could on the settee and waited for him to tell her what it was, specifically, that he didn't like about Charles.

Byron came over to her and gave her one of the glasses of water. "I wasn't sure if Charles was going to let you come here alone."

"Why not?"

"I'm sure he suspects that I've figured out why he married you," he said as he sat next to her.

"He married me because he loves me."

"I realize he made you believe he loves you, but I happen to know that's not the case."

Not in the mood for something to drink, Eris set the glass on the table. "Why do you think he married me?"

"Money," Byron replied. "It's why most gentlemen marry ladies who are wealthy."

"That's absurd. Charles has plenty of money."

"Jonathan had more. With some gentlemen, the more they get, the more they want, and sadly, no amount they acquire ever satisfies them. I think Charles saw a naïve widow who just came into a lot of money and decided to use that to his advantage."

"It didn't happen that way. Money isn't why he married me."

"You don't see things the way they really are because you've fallen in love with him." He put a comforting hand on her shoulder. "This is partly my fault. If I had any idea Charles was going to convince you to run off to Gretna Green to marry him, I wouldn't have taken the job that took me out of London for those weeks following the funeral. It's just that you've never done anything so foolhardy in the past. It took me by surprise."

She shrugged his hand away. "I'm thirty-five, Byron. What was I supposed to do? Wait a full year and then go through a courtship and have all the banns read again? Unlike gentlemen, ladies aren't able to have children whenever they want. As it is, I'll be lucky to have children at my age."

"Is that why you married him? You wanted children?"

"No. Yes. Well, it was part of it. I do want to have children, but that wasn't the reason I married him. He wanted to be with me." She pointed to herself. "Me, Byron. For the first time in my life, a gentleman actually cared about me." When her brother gave her a look that expressed how sorry he was she believed what she was saying, she added, "Charles only came by to ask if he could have something that belonged to Jonathan. That's how we started talking. There was nothing romantic in that first conversation we had. I didn't even think I was going to see him again. Then when I took Reina to the market, he happened to be there, and we talked again. And from there, we talked some more, and we just fell in love. I admit I struggled with whether it was wise to marry so soon after Jonathan's death, but when a lady gets to be my age, she doesn't feel like waiting when there's a gentleman who already loves her and wants to get married."

Byron let out a heavy sigh. "I'm so sorry, Eris. The last thing I ever wanted was for you to be hurt."

Heat rose up to her cheeks. "I don't want your pity. Charles is sincere in how he feels about me. I'm sure of it."

"My job is to know when someone is lying, and Charles is hiding something." He took a drink of his water then paused as he searched for the right words to say next. "You know I keep quiet about the reasons people hire me. Well, I'm going to break that rule because you need to know this. Someone was threatening Jonathan. I saw the missives for myself, Eris. The person seemed convinced that Jonathan owed him money. Jonathan was baffled by it. He didn't owe anyone any debts. I checked into Jonathan's life to verify he was telling the truth, and he was. Jonathan's history was impeccable. Whoever sent those missives wanted Jonathan to leave him money at secluded spots in London where the person would collect it, discreetly, of course, so no one would know about it. Jonathan refused to do it. My job was to find out who the person was." He shook his head. "I wasn't able to track the person down before Jonathan died. I think this person killed him."

Eris' eyes grew wide. "Why didn't you tell me this before?"

"There was no proof. Without proof, I can't convict someone of a crime. I still don't have proof." He set his glass next to hers then took her hands in his. "Eris, I think Charles murdered Jonathan. I think that's the secret he's hiding."

She gasped. She couldn't believe what she was hearing! "Charles and Jonathan were close friends. They'd known each other for a long time. Charles was devastated by his death. Whenever Charles talks about him, I can see the pain on his face. He never would have killed Jonathan."

"Most of the time it's the person who's close to a person who ends up being the murderer. The person can be a family member or a friend. Murderers aren't always acquaintances or strangers."

She rose to her feet. She couldn't stay here and listen to this. She just couldn't! "You're wrong, Byron. Charles doesn't have it in him to kill someone. He's a good and honorable person."

Byron stood up and stopped her before she could leave the room. "He's a good actor, Eris. He didn't marry you for love. Of that, I am certain. You need to listen to me. I don't think your life is in any danger, but I am continuing my investigation into this situation, and I don't want you to be devastated if it turns out I'm right."

"You're not right. If Jonathan was murdered, someone else did it."

When he shook his head, she pushed past him and hurried to get out of the house. She had known that talking to her brother was going to be uncomfortable, but she hadn't thought it was going to be this horrible. Imagine him accusing Charles of murdering Jonathan! There was no way she could tell Charles this. Jonathan's death had been so painful for him. This would only make things worse.

Byron followed her as she left the house.

"Eris, this is important," he said as she climbed into the carriage. He told the coachman not to leave then hopped into the carriage and closed the door. He sat next to her. Ignoring her irritated groan, he said, "It's possible Charles isn't guilty. I'll grant you that. The doctor might be right. It's possible Jonathan did die from heart failure. But it's also possible someone murdered him. In order to figure out what happened, I need you to get something for me."

Since he was willing to accept the possibility of Charles' innocence, she asked, "What do you want?"

"I told Jonathan to keep track of the places he went and the people he talked to. I asked him to get a small book to write in. This book would be small enough to fit into his pocket so he could take it with him when he left the townhouse. No one but me was supposed to know about the book. Even if the person threatening him didn't kill him, he probably came across this person without realizing it. I need to see the names of everyone in that book."

"If this book was so important, why didn't you take it when you were in his bedchamber with the doctor on the morning of Jonathan's death?"

"I couldn't find it in the bedchamber. I'm not even sure he kept a record of where he went and who he spoke to. Just in case he did, will you search for a book with those things in it and bring it to me?"

If it was going to stop Byron from blaming Charles of something he never did, she would gladly do it. "All right, I'll do that."

"Whatever you do, don't tell Charles."

She glared at him. And to think she believed he was going to open himself up to the possibility that Charles was innocent!

"If a killer suspects they've been figured out, they might panic. If they panic, they're likely to kill again to get rid of the person who suspects them of the crime. If it is Charles, and I'm not saying it is for sure, Charles might kill you. That's why you can't tell him anything. Also, you need to make sure that no one, not even a servant, sees you take the book if you happen to find it."

"I'll look for the book and bring it to you, but I'm not doing it because I believe Charles killed Jonathan. I'm doing it because I believe he didn't. I want you to investigate the situation and realize you're wrong."

"For your sake, I hope I am wrong," he said. He opened the door. "Be careful. This might be a dangerous situation."

"I'll be careful."

He gave her a nod before he left the carriage.

***

Charles walked down the street toward the market. The pearl button and Jonathan's small book were discreetly tucked away into the pocket of his coat.

He didn't know what to make of the entries Jonathan had made in the book, but there had to be something important about them. A gentleman didn't make such a meticulous record unless there was a good reason for it. Maybe Jonathan knew someone wanted to kill him.

The thought that Jonathan knew something this important but didn't bother telling him about it hurt. He thought Jonathan had trusted him with everything. There wasn't a single thing Charles ever kept from his friend.

It had nothing to do with your friendship. Jonathan was probably too scared to say anything.

Maybe Jonathan was afraid if he said anything to Charles, the killer would come after him, too.

But why would anyone want to kill Jonathan?

Charles hoped the answer would start with the identity of the person who owned the button he'd found that morning.

His steps slowed as he approached the only shop in London he knew that made buttons as elegant as the one he currently carried in his pocket. So much hinged on what the shop owner would tell him. He didn't have the faintest idea who killed Jonathan. He'd been wrong about Eris and Byron. That didn't leave him with many options left. If the answer wasn't here, he wasn't ever going to find out who murdered his friend.

He gripped the cane in his hand. He couldn't fail his friend. The answer had to be here. The button had to be the proof he'd been looking for.

He released his breath and headed into the shop. The shop contained luxuries that enhanced a gentleman's wardrobe. In addition to buttons, there were tie pins, jabots, premium gloves, and canes.

At the moment, the owner was speaking with a customer, so Charles chose to scan the collection of buttons. There was a surprising variety of them. Jonathan hadn't had anything like these on his clothes. Charles took the button out of his pocket and, fortunately, the elaborate work done on some of the other buttons in front of him matched the quality of work done on the one he was holding.

Charles glanced over at the gentleman who was speaking with the owner. Charles didn't recognize him. He was a younger gentleman. The gentleman made a comment about wanting to purchase an accessory that would best attract ladies. "I want to let them know I have sufficient money but not too much," the gentleman said. "My father warned me it would be best to let my outfits express my wealth rather than coming out and saying I have money."

"Your father is a wise gentleman," the owner replied. "Most of the time, how we present ourselves is more important than what we say." The owner glanced at Charles. "I'll be with you in a moment."

Charles indicated he could wait then turned his attention back to the buttons. He was certain the pearl button he was holding had been made here. There was no other shop in London that made anything so fine. Or expensive.

Who did Jonathan know that had so much money he could waste it on buttons? Charles considered himself to be well off. Jonathan had been more so. But neither he nor Jonathan had the kind of money to waste on buttons. This was a shop that only the richest in London could afford. It catered to the likes of Lord Edon and Lord Valentine.

Who else in London had this kind of wealth who would be capable of murder? Just as he was about to pull the book out of his pocket, the owner came over to him.

"I'm sorry for making you wait," the owner said. "How may I help you?"

"I was wondering if you made this button." Charles held the button out to him.

The owner took it and nodded. "Yes, I made a set of these."

Encouraged, Charles straightened up. "Do you remember the gentleman who bought it? I found it while I was taking a walk, and since it's such an exquisite button, I wanted to give it to the gentleman it belongs to."

"It fell off his waistcoat? I assured him that when I sewed my buttons on clothing, they never come off. Oh dear." He went over to the counter and pulled out a hardbound ledger. "I feel terrible about this. I really do my best to secure my buttons so this kind of thing doesn't happen."

"I'm sure it wasn't your fault."

"That's nice of you to say, but it is." He turned the pages of the ledger until he came to the one he was looking for. "I sold this button to Lord Hemmington."

Charles' ears perked up. He was sure he saw that name in the book, but he had to look at it again to be sure.

The owner reached for a piece of parchment and wrote on it. "When you see Lord Hemmington, would you please express my apologies? I want to make up for this incident. Tell him I'll gift him another set of buttons, and I'll make sure those are secure."

"I'll give him the message."

"Thank you. Here is his address. He can stop in at any time for the new buttons."

Relieved it was going to be this easy, Charles took the parchment and button then left the shop.

He waited until he was a couple of blocks from the shop before he sat on a bench. He put the cane next to him then took the book out of his pocket. He tucked the button into another pocket and then opened the book. He scanned through all of the entries, and on the third page, he found what he was looking for: *Lord Hemmington*. So he was right. Jonathan had talked with him.

He turned the pages. It looked like Jonathan had spoken with him a total of three times. One of them had been the day before he died. Charles forced down the lump in his throat. Now wasn't the time to think of that final day, or the last time he had spoken with Jonathan himself. He had plenty of time to do that later.

He took a look at the parchment and noted the location of Lord Hemmington's townhouse. It wasn't in the same place Jonathan had met him. Jonathan had talked to him at Aldercy's Club. Charles didn't know much about the gentleman's establishment except that it wasn't like White's which was exclusive. Anyone could go to Aldercy's as long as they had a certain amount of wealth. If Charles remembered right, he hadn't had enough two years ago when Jonathan tried to talk him into giving it a try. But his marriage to Eris might have changed that.

Charles glanced at the parchment. Which would be a better place to go? Should he try the townhouse or Aldercy's first?

He tapped the parchment on the book. He should try the club first. Charles needed to be careful. The store owner believed he had found the button while walking in London, but Lord Hemmington would probably know differently. He'd been wearing the waistcoat the night he killed Jonathan. There was no way to know if he realized that button had come off while in the bedchamber or not.

Charles' guess was that he hadn't. He'd probably been too worried about placing Jonathan's body on the bed so it looked as if he'd suffered a heart attack. The room had been neat and in order. Even Eris hadn't heard anything from her bedchamber. Lord Hemmington had been careful to be quiet, and he'd made it look like he hadn't been there. No one suspected the truth. Not the doctor. Not the Runner. Not the constable when Charles went to him about his concerns.

It was the perfect crime.

Charles folded the parchment and put it in his pocket. He couldn't go to Lord Hemmington with the story about finding the button. That had worked for the shop owner, but it wouldn't work for him. Charles had to come up with a different strategy.

He tucked the book into his pocket and went through his options.

Aldercy's was a public place. If Lord Hemmington was there, Charles could go up to him and start a conversation. He had to figure out how Lord Hemmington knew Jonathan. He would have to be subtle.

Maybe he'd just start with a question about buttons. Then he would take it from there. Maybe he'd find a way to work Jonathan into the conversation, and maybe Lord Hemmington would say something that would give Charles the reason why Lord Hemmington had killed him. Then Charles could go to the constable with the reason and the evidence, and finally, at long last, the murderer would be held accountable for what he'd done.

Excited, Charles took the cane that was resting next to him and headed for Aldercy's.

Chapter Twenty

Eris spent almost an hour searching through Charles' entire bedchamber, but she didn't find the book her brother had told her about. She groaned in frustration. Byron was never going to believe Charles was innocent without that book.

Maybe it wasn't in the bedchamber. Maybe it was in the library. She had her books in her bedchamber, but Jonathan kept his in the library. She remembered going in there to get the ledger for the steward to manage after his death since she didn't know the first thing about finances. She assumed Charles took over that aspect of things once he married her, but she hadn't thought to ask. All she knew was that she had a set allowance each week, and it was more than what Byron had been able to give her.

When she got to the library, she searched through the room but didn't see anything that resembled the kind of book Byron had told her about. She put down the last book and sat in the chair.

She didn't know what she was going to do. All she could do was tell Byron the book wasn't here. She could implore him to believe her when she said Charles didn't murder Jonathan, but if he hadn't accepted her words before, how could she expect him to accept them the next time they spoke to each other?

A soft knock came at the open door of the library. She turned her attention to the butler.

"Miss Livingstone is here," he said. "Are you available for visitors?"

Glad for the reprieve, Eris rose to her feet. "Yes. I'll meet her in the drawing room. Please bring us tea and queen cakes."

With a nod, he left the room.

Eris gave one more look around the room, and as she expected, the small book didn't magically appear anywhere. Shoulders slumped, she went to the drawing room.

As soon as Reina saw her, she hurried over to give her a hug. "I thought you could use a friend to talk to."

Eris hugged her back. "Thank you. You're right. I could."

Reina let go of her and led her to the settee where the two sat. "I have no idea what was happening between Charles and Byron, but I could tell it ruined your evening. How are you feeling today?"

"Worse than I felt last night." She made sure none of the servants were nearby before adding, "As you know my brother is a Runner. He's in the habit of figuring out who committed a crime. These can be anything from a small theft to something more serious like murder. Well, he—" Eris' voice choked on the next word, so she had to stop herself and wait until she could speak clearly. "He thinks Charles murdered Jonathan."

Reina's eyes grew wide. "He thinks my cousin killed his nearest and dearest friend?"

Eris fought back her tears. "I don't know what to do. Charles isn't a killer."

"No, he's not. My cousin doesn't have it in him to harm anyone."

"I know he doesn't. I explained that to my brother this morning, but he refuses to believe me." She checked the doorway again to make sure no one was there then added, "I thought my brother was upset that I married so soon after Jonathan's death or that he just didn't like Charles. It didn't occur to me that he would accuse Charles of murder."

"Did he say why he thought that?"

"Money. He thinks Charles saw an opportunity to get more money if he murdered his friend and then married me. He has this idea in his mind that Charles is only pretending to be in love with me."

"I can assure you that Charles' feelings are sincere. He came to me shortly after the funeral to ask if I would befriend you so that he could get better acquainted with you. I wasn't supposed to say anything because he wanted everything to seem like it all happened by chance. But it was all by design. He secretly admired you before I even met you."

"So you weren't lost the day we met?"

Reina offered her an apologetic smile. "Charles dropped me off a few townhouses from here and told me which one to go to. I hope you aren't upset. I really do like you. You did become a good friend."

Eris returned her smile. "I'm not upset. Actually, I'm flattered."

Imagine a gentleman going to such lengths in order to be with her. As Reina had pointed out, they were friends now. All turned out well in the end. Also, it did bring forth something important that neither she nor Byron had known.

"Maybe that's what Byron is talking about when he told me Charles is hiding something," Eris said. "My brother was insistent that Charles wasn't telling me something."

"I can't think of what else it could be. It has to be the plan he came up with so that he could get to know you better."

Yes, that had to be it. All of it made sense in light of this new information.

The butler came into the room with a tray and set it on the table in front of them.

Reina waited until he left before saying, "Tell your brother how you and I really met. I think that will reassure him that Charles isn't a murderer."

"I will."

Already, she felt much better. Once she and Reina were done with their visit, she would go to Byron's residence and tell him what she had discovered. Then, hopefully, they could put this whole thing behind them.

***

As Charles went through Aldercy's, he paid close attention to the buttons on the gentlemen's clothing. There were two who had elaborate buttons that reminded him of the work the shop owner did. One was at a gaming table playing cards, and the other was reading a newspaper in the corner of the room.

He tapped the top of Jonathan's cane for several long moments before he decided to approach the gentleman who was reading.

The gentleman glanced up at him.

"Forgive the interruption," Charles said. "Are you Lord Hemmington?"

The gentleman shook his head. "The gentleman you're looking for is over there." He pointed to the one who was at the card table.

"Thank you," Charles replied. "I'm sorry I interrupted you."

Out of courtesy, the gentleman assured him it was fine.

Charles turned and went over to the tables. He remained to the side so as not to interrupt anyone in the middle of a game. When the game came to an end, Charles walked up to him.

Lord Hemmington collected the money he'd won and glanced over at Charles.

"Are you Lord Hemmington?" Charles asked.

Lord Hemmington frowned. "Do I owe you money?"

"No," Charles replied, surprised that should be the first thing he'd say to him. "The matter I wish to discuss has nothing to do with money."

Lord Hemmington put the money into his pocket and then excused himself from the table.

Charles followed him to a vacant corner of the room and sat in the chair next to him. "It's a simple matter. I won't take up much of your time. I was just at the market, and I came across a shop that specializes in accessories for gentlemen's clothing. The owner there said you can attest to the quality of his work. I'm thinking of buying buttons from him, but I want to make sure the price he charges is worth it. The amount he asks is a little on the excessive side."

"Are you referring to Mr. Clancy?"

"Yes, that's the owner's name."

"Am I the only person he named?"

"You're the first name that came up," Charles replied, hoping the gentleman wouldn't ask for a list of the other gentlemen the owner had mentioned. That would give away his lie if he had to make someone up who didn't do business at that shop. Charles' grip tightened on the cane as he waited for the gentleman to respond.

Lord Hemmington's gaze went to the cane. "That cane looks familiar. Did you buy it from Mr. Clancy?"

"No, but then, I didn't see any canes in his shop when I was there today," Charles said. "Did he used to sell canes?"

"The last time I went to see him, there were a couple of handcrafted canes on display. That's a nice cane. I wouldn't mind one from someone who crafted that. Where did you get it from?"

Charles hesitated to answer. Lord Hemmington's button had been in Jonathan's bedchamber. If he came out and said it belonged to Jonathan, then Lord Hemmington would know he had figured out he'd murdered his friend. Charles quickly thought of another answer and said, "It was a gift from my family. They thought it would make me more stylish."

Lord Hemmington nodded. "They're right. It does. The work on it is exquisite. Some might even say it's unforgettable. Unforgettable things are important." He smiled then added, "Mr. Clancy is skilled at what he does. I recommend him if you're serious about getting those buttons. Do you have any other questions for me?"

Charles couldn't be sure, but he thought there was something underlying the gentleman's tone that indicated he wasn't the least bit pleased Charles had bothered him. Charles struggled to understand what he had done to annoy him, but nothing came to mind. Charles had been careful not to mention Jonathan or finding the button. He'd given Lord Hemmington no clues that he had deducted the truth about Jonathan's death. And yet, a prickling sensation in the back of his mind told him he had made an error somewhere along the way.

"Um, no," Charles forced out. "I only came to ask about the buttons."

"I'm glad I could be of assistance." Lord Hemmington rose from the chair and went back to the gaming tables.

Charles waited for a couple of seconds before he got up and left the establishment. He had to talk to the constable. He had to let the constable know he knew who killed Jonathan, and he would show him the button and Mr. Clancy's note as proof. With a glance to make sure the street was clear, he hurried across it and went in the direction of the constable's residence.

Chapter Twenty-One

"You don't honestly believe that, do you?" Byron asked Eris an hour later when she went to visit him.

"Why would I have a reason to doubt Reina?" Eris replied.

Byron leaned back in the settee and rolled his eyes. "Charles wasn't secretly in love with you, Eris. He had another reason for talking his naïve cousin into befriending you."

"What other reason could there be?"

"Money."

"Charles didn't marry me for money." If only Eris had been able to find that book! But what if Jonathan hadn't kept a book that recorded where he went and whom he talked to? What if Byron had suggested it but Jonathan hadn't done it? "I looked all over the townhouse, but I couldn't find a small book that Jonathan wrote in. Can't you just believe me when I say that Charles isn't a murderer?"

"I believe facts. I believe evidence. I'm sorry, Eris, but how you feel can't be the basis on which I make a judgment in this situation."

"But Reina told me he set things up so that he could get better acquainted with me. Do you think Reina is lying?"

He shook his head. "No, I don't. My instincts tell me that Reina was as deceived as you were. Charles is the one who's hiding something."

"I already told you what it was."

"I realize you and Reina believe that story, but Charles wasn't hiding the fact that he secretly admired you from afar. That's only the kind of thing you'll read in love stories. Gentlemen don't go around plotting ways to get into a lady's company because they've fallen in love with her. They just go up and start talking to her."

"Not everyone is as bold as you are. Some people are shyer than you, and Charles is one of those people."

"Charles is not shy. You're mistaking his silence for shyness." When she groaned, he added, "How long have I been a Runner?"

"Fifteen years."

"As of last month, it's been sixteen years. I know what I'm doing, Eris. I'm not a novice at this. My instincts are right. Charles is hiding something, and it's important you're careful around him. If he suspects you might have figured out what he's doing, you could suffer the same fate Jonathan did."

"He didn't kill Jonathan! Jonathan was his friend." How many times did she have to say this? Accusing Charles of lying to her and Reina about the secret admiration part was one thing, but she refused—absolutely refused!—to accept the premise that Charles had murdered Jonathan.

"Then let me investigate things for myself," Byron said. "Let me into the townhouse. I'll see what I can find."

"There's nothing to find. I told you that there is no book."

"There might be something else."

"If I let you search the townhouse, will you stop accusing Charles of murder?"

"Only if I'm convinced he didn't do it."

That was as good as nothing. Her not finding a book hadn't been enough. What made her think that finding nothing else would get her brother to stop this nonsense?

"Please, Eris. Let me into the townhouse. I need to do a thorough search of the place. What I'm looking for could be outside Jonathan's bedchamber."

"I don't know. It doesn't seem like it'll do any good."

"It might make the difference for your safety."

"Charles isn't going to hurt me. He loves me."

"What is the harm in letting me search the place so I can be sure of that?"

It should be enough for her to tell him that Charles wasn't a murderer. She wondered if he would believe her if she was a gentleman. While he'd never made her feel like she was daft because she was a lady before, she was beginning to feel that way now.

But if she didn't let him search through the townhouse, things might get worse. He might start following Charles around or start doing things to seriously antagonize Charles. Maybe if she let him go through the townhouse, he would find nothing—because there would be nothing to find—and then relent.

"All right," she consented. "Come with me if you want to look through the townhouse." She stood up and gave him an expectant look.

He rose to his feet. "Thank you. I won't be long. I know where I need to search. I'll get my hat and coat, and we'll be on our way."

She sighed and waited for him to get ready to go to her townhouse.

***

The constable set the button and the note on his desk. With a shake of his head, he said, "These don't prove anything."

"Why not?" Charles asked.

"Because anyone could lose a button for any reason in any location. I was there the morning Jonathan's body was discovered. As you requested, I searched the bedchamber. This button wasn't there."

"That button was under Jonathan's dresser," Charles said. "It was pressed up against the floor and the wall. It was easy to miss."

"I didn't see it."

"Just because you didn't see it, it doesn't mean it wasn't there. Even I missed it when I searched through the bedchamber. I only found it this morning."

The constable paused for almost a minute before saying, "It isn't my intention to upset you, but is it possible that this button came off at some point after Jonathan's death? Jonathan's widow might have had a gentleman visit her."

Charles stiffened. "She would never do such a thing. She's not that kind of lady."

"Then I am forced to make another conclusion, and you'll like this one even less."

Charles couldn't imagine what could be worse than the constable accusing his dear and lovely wife of sharing a bed with someone she wasn't married to, but he asked, "What other conclusion can there be?"

"It's possible that you can't accept the fact that your friend died of natural causes. I understand the friendship you two shared was important to you. No one likes to discuss death. Even though it's something we all eventually face, it's a very ugly reality. We spend our lives pretending it'll never happen to us or those we cherish. Given Jonathan's age, I propose that you convinced yourself he was murdered."

Charles couldn't believe what he was hearing! "I'm not an unreasonable gentleman. I'm well aware that people of all ages die. What I know is that Jonathan was healthy. He didn't have an illness. He wasn't sickly."

"Death can be sudden. Not everyone has a warning it's going to happen."

Charles closed his eyes so he wouldn't start yelling. When he opened them, he felt more in control of his emotions. "That button was under the dresser. Someone snuck into Jonathan's bedchamber and killed him." He picked up the button and showed it to the constable. "This is an expensive button. It's not something most gentlemen wear on their clothing. Jonathan didn't buy buttons like this. You, the doctor, and I don't buy buttons like this. Servants don't buy buttons like this. The one person Jonathan knew who wears buttons like this is Lord Hemmington. I verified that by talking to the person who makes these buttons. Why is that not sufficient proof?"

"It's not sufficient proof because no one saw it under the dresser on the day Jonathan's body was discovered. We don't know if that button rolled under the dresser until days or weeks later. And, as much as I hate to say it, you're the only person saying this button was under the dresser."

Inspired, Charles said, "My wife saw it, too. She was with me when I found it."

"How am I supposed to assume you didn't put it there and waited until she was there to discover it with you?"

"I have no reason to do something like that."

The constable studied him. "I don't know what to think. There's no proof of murder, but it is strange that you're insistent your friend was killed."

Charles didn't like the way this conversation was going. This wasn't what he expected when he came here. "Are you suggesting I murdered my friend?" he asked in shock.

"No, I don't believe you killed him." Before Charles could breathe a sigh of relief, he added, "I don't believe your friend was murdered. That button might have been under the dresser for a short time or for a long time. It's impossible to say."

"What if I go back to the shop and ask Mr. Clancy when he made it?"

"Then all we would know is when he made a button for Lord Hemmington. We wouldn't know when the button ended up under the dresser. This is all conjecture." His expression turned sympathetic. "I'm sorry. I know this isn't what you want to hear, but there's no judge who will accept the premise of this case. My advice is for you to give up this pursuit. It's going to get you nowhere. Live your life. Enjoy the people around you who are still living. Embrace the blessings you have."

"But Lord Hemmington killed my friend. Am I supposed to just let him get away with it?"

"If Lord Hemmington murdered Jonathan—and I don't believe he did—there isn't enough proof to convict him of the crime."

Charles thought for a long moment then asked, "What if Mr. Clancy only made this specific button for Lord Hemmington? What if this is the only one like this in all of London?"

"That would get closer to what you're looking for, but it still doesn't mean Lord Hemmington was there on the evening of Jonathan's death. It also doesn't mean Lord Hemmington was in the house for Jonathan. He could be a secret lover of the lady you just married."

"I know for a fact she has no lovers, and she can tell you that as well."

"And if Lord Hemmington says she was his lover, what then? Or what if your wife is lying so a scandal doesn't erupt? What if Lord Hemmington let Jonathan borrow his coat? There are many possibilities that still lead us to the same conclusion we are at now."

In other words, the constable wasn't going to help him. Charles was on his own. And sadly, he had so little to go by. Just how was he supposed to find definitive proof when one conversation with Lord Hemmington had shown Charles that he made a poor detective? Charles still couldn't get rid of the feeling that he'd made a mistake somewhere along the way when he was talking to the gentleman. He just couldn't figure out what the mistake was, and without knowing that, how could he correct for it if he spoke to him again?

"I truly am sorry about your friend's death," the constable said. "Maybe it will help if you went to his grave. Have a conversation with him. Tell him the things you didn't get to say while he was alive. Some people find that helps after losing a loved one. And, something to keep in mind, is that death is only a temporary separation. There is a life after this. You will see him again."

Charles' shoulders slumped forward in defeat. So that was it. Even though he had found out who killed his friend, there was nothing he could do. The murderer was going to go free, wasting his days at gaming tables in a gentleman's club, and there was nothing—nothing at all—that Charles could do about it.

***

Eris stood up from the settee when she saw Byron enter the drawing room. Byron shut the doors, and at once, she knew she wasn't going to like what he was going to say.

"Charles didn't do it," she said. "Whatever you think, you're wrong."

His expression grim, he walked over to her. "You need to act prudently."

"I can't believe what I'm hearing. Charles is not a murderer."

"Eris, he had locks put in his bedchamber. He put a lock in the door leading to the small room off to the side of the bedchamber, he put a lock on the door connecting your bedchamber with his, and he put a lock on the door that connects the bedchamber to the hallway. Jonathan didn't have locks. Don't you find that even a little suspicious?"

"He's probably a private person. Maybe he's afraid the servants will come in unexpectedly."

Byron gave her a skeptical look. "I know you're trying to hold onto the hope that he's innocent, but at some point, you have to accept the evidence that's right in front of you."

"How are locks on some doors evidence that he killed Jonathan?"

"It's not evidence he's a murderer, but he is hiding something."

She was tempted to remind him about the things Reina had told her, but what good would it do? He had it set in his mind that Charles had married her for the money instead of the fact that he loved her. An idea popped in her head, so she asked, "If he did marry me for money, then why would he put locks on his doors? The money isn't in his bedchamber."

"That's where things fall apart."

Encouraged, she said, "Then you can't conclude anything bad about him, can you?"

"Something is wrong. I know it. There's been something wrong this entire time ever since Jonathan's death, and I haven't been able to figure it out. I've never had something I couldn't solve before. Jonathan came to me because he was receiving threatening missives, and he was sure someone was following him."

"Maybe those things were really happening, and he died anyway. It is possible."

"Possible but not likely."

Maybe if she'd been brave enough, she would have gone to Jonathan on their wedding night. Then she would have been there when he died, and she could verify no one had murdered him.

But did any newly married lady go to her husband's bedchamber? Eris was under the impression that it was the bride's responsibility to wait for the bridegroom to come to her.

She sighed. "I don't know what to tell you, Byron. The last time I saw Jonathan was when he escorted me to my bedchamber. He said he would be with me soon." She hesitated to add more since it was private, but if it was going to convince him that Charles wasn't a bad person, then being more forthcoming with personal matters would be worth it. "Halfway into the night, I began to think that he changed his mind. I cried for a while because I thought he didn't really want to be with me and then I fell asleep. When I woke up, the servants were talking about finding him dead. It never once occurred to me to check on him at any point in the night to see if he was alive."

"No one would have expected you to do that. No one expected him to die. I thought the person who was threatening him only wanted to scare him. Gentlemen give out threats all the time. Rarely does anyone die as a result."

After a moment, a thought came to her. "What if Charles put the locks on those doors because he was scared?"

"If you're suggesting he's been receiving threatening missives or has someone following him, you're wrong."

"No, I wasn't suggesting that." Her eyebrows furrowed. "How can you be sure he's not receiving any threatening missives or being followed?"

He closed his mouth and gave her that stonelike look he'd had when they used to play a game where she had to figure out where he had hidden something.

She gasped. "Have you been following him?"

He didn't answer right away, but when he did, he admitted, "I got suspicious when I came by to visit you and found out you had eloped with him."

"That's why you seemed to show up out of nowhere on the day we returned to London. You've been keeping a watch over this townhouse."

"You're my sister, Eris. It's my responsibility to make sure you're safe."

She couldn't believe it. "You spent all this time trying to convince me that Charles is hiding a horrible secret when you've been investigating him."

"Any brother in my position would have done the same thing. I'm not going to apologize for doing what's right."

She crossed her arms. "All right then. Since you've been following him, what have you found out that I need to know?"

He sighed. "Nothing, unfortunately. Charles has nothing remotely interesting going on in his life."

She glared at him.

"Except for you, of course," her brother added. "If there was something interesting going on before your marriage to him, I missed it. I never imagined you would marry so soon after Jonathan's death."

"Well, you've searched through the townhouse and didn't find anything to make you think he's a horrible person, so can you at least stop treating Charles as if he's a criminal?"

"I can't promise you that as long as my instincts are warning me that something isn't right."

She groaned. "I don't know what to tell you, Byron. I've run out of patience. I've done everything you asked. Charles loves me. He didn't marry me for money, and he didn't murder Jonathan. Whatever your instincts are telling you, it can't be that Charles did something wrong."

"What I know is that he's somehow involved in something."

She couldn't take it anymore. She just couldn't! She stormed to the doors of the drawing room and flung them open. "I want you to leave. I need some time away from you."

She was afraid he was going to argue with her, but, thankfully, he headed for the doorway.

Before he crossed the threshold, he paused and turned to her. "Please don't tell anyone about our conversations today."

She stared at him in disbelief. "Are you worried Charles won't like you if I do?"

"No. I don't care if he likes me or not. My job isn't to be liked. My job is to solve crimes. There's no telling what will happen if Charles finds out anything I've told you today."

"I can't keep this from him forever."

"Then keep this to yourself for the next few weeks. I'll make a deal with you." He lowered his voice. "One month. Give me one month to do some more investigating. In that time, if I still can't reach any conclusions, you can tell Charles everything."

"I hate keeping something like this from him."

"I know you do, but I have to make sure you're safe. Just in case Charles isn't the person you think he is, you have to be careful. Someone who has something to hide can become violent if they suspect they've been discovered."

"You've already told me that."

"I'm telling you again so you'll be careful. Do this for me because I'm your brother. You're the only family I have left, Eris. I couldn't bear it if something bad happened to you."

"I'll give you one month," she agreed. "But that's all I'm doing, Byron. After that, you have to put this whole thing behind you."

"I will. A month is all I need." He gave her a kiss on the cheek. "I'll speak with you soon."

She offered him a nod then watched as he left.

Chapter Twenty-Two

Charles lost track of time as he stood in front of Jonathan's grave. As much as he wished there was something he could do, he had exhausted all of his options. Though he'd figured out who murdered Jonathan, he couldn't do anything about it. Lord Hemmington was going to get away with it.

"I wish you were here," Charles whispered.

Even as he said the words, he knew if Jonathan was here, it would mean he never would have married Eris. And if he hadn't married her, he wouldn't have fallen in love with her, and if he hadn't fallen in love with her, he would have missed out on one of the best things that had ever happened to him.

He didn't know how to reconcile the contradiction. He missed Jonathan so much. He wanted Jonathan to be standing next to him so he could talk to him again. At least one more time.

Charles wiped his eyes with the handkerchief then tucked it into his pocket. He had to get home. Eris would be wondering where he was. He'd spent almost the whole day running around.

He turned from the grave and headed home. The tapping of the cane and his footsteps seemed hollow on the sidewalk. He made himself greet everyone with a smile as they passed him by, even though smiling was the last thing he felt like doing. It was amazing how people could pretend that everything was all right when it wasn't.

He entered the townhouse and searched for Eris. It turned out she was reading a book in the drawing room. When she noticed him, she set the book aside and rose to her feet.

He went over to her. "I'm sorry I was gone for so long."

"Are you all right?"

He didn't want to burden her with everything he'd learned, especially since there was nothing he could do about it, so he just said, "I visited Jonathan's grave. It felt appropriate to say good-bye to him." He thought of the funeral then added, "Again." He glanced at the clock. " I was gone much longer than I meant to be. I didn't realize I missed dinner."

"Do you want me to have Cook make you something?"

"No, I'm too tired to eat."

She hugged him. "I know you miss Jonathan. You were such good friends."

He opened his mouth to respond, but a sob rose up in his throat. He managed to force it down before she pulled away from him. The last thing he wanted to do was cry in front of another person, even if that person was his wife.

"I think I'll go to Jonathan's favorite room and sit there for a while," he said. "You don't mind if I do that, do you?"

"Of course not."

He kissed her then caressed her cheek. "I'll be a better husband to you tomorrow."

"You're already a better husband, Charles. I didn't know Jonathan as well as you did, but I understand you need time alone to grieve his passing. No one can expect you to go on as if nothing happened." She reached up to take his hand in hers and squeezed it. "Take as much time as you need."

She offered him a smile that gave him more comfort than anything else had that day.

He thanked her and left the drawing room. He turned down the hall and headed for the library. Once there, he shut the door and scanned the room. It was hard to believe he was never going to sit in here and visit with Jonathan again. They'd never discuss the books they'd read or play a game of chess in the corner of the room. They'd never even just sit and talk about what was happening in London. Every time he came in here, it would only be him.

He trudged over to the desk, plopped into the chair, and set the cane next to him. He'd never felt more defeated in his entire life. He had not only lost his friend, but he'd failed him as well.

He took out the small book from his pocket and the button. So much for these things. They hadn't done him any good. He placed both on the desk then leaned back in the chair and closed his eyes.

He thought of the first time he'd come by to visit Jonathan in this townhouse. He and Jonathan had known each other since they were fifteen, but Jonathan was eighteen when he purchased this place. And the very first room Jonathan had taken him to was this one.

"You ought to move out of your parents' townhouse," Jonathan told him that day. "Get your own townhouse to live in."

"I don't have that kind of money," Charles replied. "I wasn't born in a tower of gold like you were."

"I wasn't born in a tower of gold." After a pause, he added, "It was more like a mountain."

"Yes, well, someday I might have more than you since I'm a better investor."

Jonathan pretended to shiver as if the prospect frightened him.

Charles felt a chuckle rise up in his throat at the memory.

Then his mind went to a time when he had discovered a new chess strategy he wanted to try out, and it had been so successful that he managed to beat

Jonathan in four consecutive games. Try as he might, Jonathan couldn't figure out the strategy Charles was using.

"Won't you give me a hint?" Jonathan asked.

"If I do that, you'll win," Charles replied.

"Well, if I don't figure out your secret, I'll never win another game."

"That wouldn't bother me."

Jonathan gave him an exasperated sigh. After a moment, he asked, "What is the fun of winning if there's no challenge in it for you? As it is, this game is much too easy."

"The fun will be in watching you squirm as you try to figure out how I'm winning all the time."

Though Jonathan tried to look serious, the slight smile on his face betrayed him.

"If I told you, you'd hate me for it," Charles said. "You like the challenge. I know you do, even if you won't come out and admit it."

Jonathan remained silent for a moment then said, "I'll make a wager with you. We'll play this game four more times. If I don't figure out your strategy, I'll give you my cane."

"The cane? Isn't that your favorite possession?"

"It is, so it'll give me a good reason to figure out how you're winning so easily."

"All right. You have a deal."

Charles then thought back to the last time they'd been in this room. It was the day before Jonathan got married, and though Charles wasn't prone to express his feelings, he hadn't been able to hide the fact that he wasn't all that happy about the upcoming marriage.

"I know it's selfish," Charles admitted as he sat across from Jonathan. "But I keep wondering how things will change. With your wife around, I can't just come over whenever I want. You're bound to stop coming over to my townhouse as often as you do now. Once gentlemen marry, their lives are never the same." Unable to look at him, Charles added, "You're not even married yet, and I miss you."

"It's true that we won't see each other as much," Jonathan said in a tone that let Charles know he didn't think less of him because Charles was talking in a way gentlemen weren't encouraged to. "But just because I'm getting married, it doesn't mean we'll stop being friends. You're still welcome to come here, and I'll still visit you. You're the only one who reads the same boring old books I do."

"The books aren't boring," Charles argued.

"They're boring to everyone but us. I can't think of a single other person who wants to read about the development of languages."

"I really liked learning how Latin changed into other languages."

"Yes, I did, too. But I assure you that very few gentlemen do. I guarantee you that my wife won't find any such books interesting, either. Nor will she be inclined to attend lectures with me or discuss investments. She also has no inclination to learn chess, so she'll never challenge my chess skills the way you do. I will have to continuously bear with all the strategies you come up with to confound me." Then he rolled his eyes in a way that always made Charles laugh.

Even now, Charles laughed. But with the laughter, came the piercing reality that he was never going to get another chance to see his friend roll his eyes like that again. A sob rose up in his throat, and this time, he gave into it and let himself cry.

It hurt.

It hurt so much to be without his friend that he could barely stand it. There wasn't any friend in this world as good as Jonathan. A hole was in his life that could never be filled. He didn't know how he was supposed to go on.

Charles leaned forward until his forehead was on the desk. Then he wept. He missed Jonathan so much, and there was no way he could bring him back. He knew he was going to see him again in the afterlife, but that reassurance did little to ease the pain he was going through now. This life just wasn't going to be the same without him.

He thought he heard a sound behind him, so he lifted his head from the desk. Before he could turn back, someone put a cloth over his nose and mouth. The cloth didn't smell like anything, but it was so thick that he couldn't breathe.

Charles brought his hands up to try to pry the man's hands from his face, but the man's grip was too strong. Charles fell off the chair in an attempt to get an advantage, and it worked. However, before Charles could call out for help, the man rolled him over onto his back, pinned him down, and forced the cloth back over his nose and mouth.

"Do you take me for a fool?" Lord Hemmington hissed. "I know that cane belonged to the Duke of Jowett. He took it with him to Aldercy's all the time."

Charles struggled to get Lord Hemmington off of him, but all he ended up doing was grasping at the buttons on the gentleman's frock coat.

Lord Hemmington forced the cloth down harder on Charles' face. Charles couldn't even get a little bit of air into his lungs, and he was unable to make any noise to get help.

This was it. He was going to die the same way his poor friend did. Everyone was going to assume he also died from heart failure. Lord Hemmington was going to erase any evidence that'd he'd been here. And as it was with Jonathan, no one would know the truth of his death.

Just as Charles' lungs burned to the point where he didn't think he could take it anymore, someone pulled Lord Hemmington off of him. Charles gasped in the air. His lungs stung. He coughed and struggled to breathe. Though the cloth was no longer preventing him from doing so, his body seemed to believe it was. After what seemed like a very long time but probably was only a few seconds, he finally managed to successfully take in a deep breath.

As soon as he became aware of the sound of a ruckus, he forced himself to get to his feet.

Byron slammed Lord Hemmington into a bookcase. Books went falling to the floor, but Lord Hemmington maintained his balance and gave Byron a swift punch to the jaw. Byron stumbled back but quickly recovered and sent a punch to Lord Hemmington's stomach.

Charles grabbed Jonathan's cane and left the desk.

Lord Hemmington grabbed Byron by the coat and threw him to the floor. Byron landed against a table and sent the chessboard flying across the room. Lord Hemmington got ready to pounce on him when Charles struck Lord Hemmington on the back of the head with the cane. Lord Hemmington let out a grunt and fell to the floor in an unconscious heap.

The library room door flung open, and Eris and two servants ran into the room.

Charles took a step back, and though he was slightly out of breath, he said, "Lord Hemmington came in to attack me. Byron was helping me."

The footman and butler hurried to Byron and helped him up while Eris ran over to him. "Why was he trying to attack you and my brother?"

Charles gestured to Lord Hemmington. "He killed Jonathan, and I figured it out. I don't know why your brother showed up, but if he hadn't, I'd be dead right now."

Byron walked over to them but directed his gaze to Charles. "You know Jonathan was murdered?"

"I knew he didn't die from heart failure like everyone else assumed," Charles told him.

"I knew he didn't die from heart failure, too," Byron said. "I just didn't know who murdered him."

"I didn't figure it out until today." Glad someone finally believed him, Charles waved him and Eris to the desk. "Eris and I found that button under the dresser in Jonathan's bedchamber this morning. I took that button to Mr. Clancy's shop and found out that he made it for Lord Hemmington. Then I noted that Jonathan had recorded seeing Lord Hemmington at Aldercy's."

"This is the book I've been looking for." Byron picked it up from the table. "Jonathan came to me because someone was threatening him. The person wanted money."

That explained why Lord Hemmington had asked Charles if he had owed him money earlier that day. Lord Hemmington must have lost money to Jonathan, and judging by the fact that Lord Hemmington killed him, he must have lost a substantial amount.

"Jonathan hired me to figure out who was threatening him," Byron continued. "I asked him to keep a journal of his activities." He opened it up and scanned it. "This is everything I asked him to record."

Charles put his arm around Eris and leaned into her. "I had no idea someone was threatening my friend. He didn't say anything about it."

"That's because I warned him not to," Byron replied. "Anyone could have been threatening him. I had to be careful." He sighed in regret. "It turns out I wasn't careful enough."

"You did all you could," Eris said. "Even a Runner can't get everything right."

While Eris meant well, Charles knew that was very little consolation to her brother.

Byron picked up the button and closed the book. "I'll see to it that Lord Hemmington is put in prison."

Charles released Eris and followed Byron as he walked over to Lord Hemmington, who was still unconscious. "Will anyone believe you when you tell them Lord Hemmington killed Jonathan?"

"They'll believe me because you're going to help me. With what happened this evening, there's enough evidence to convict him."

Yes, he was probably right. Between the two of them, any constable or judge would have to believe them. He ordered the servants to get the carriage ready.

After the servants left, Charles turned his attention back to Byron. "Lord Hemmington saw me with Jonathan's cane today when I asked him if Mr. Clancy made good buttons. I knew I'd made a mistake somewhere in that conversation, but I didn't realize the mistake was taking Jonathan's cane with me."

"It's often something small and insignificant that gets a criminal's attention," Byron replied.

"How did you know he was coming here? Did you see me go to Aldercy's today?"

"No, it was nothing as easy as that." He glanced at Eris who hadn't come over to them and whispered, "I thought you murdered Jonathan in order to get to the money my sister inherited. I've been keeping watch over this townhouse since I discovered Eris went missing. That was right after she left for Gretna Green."

For a moment, Charles was appalled that anyone would accuse him of murder, but then he laughed. "You won't believe this, but for a while, I thought you were the killer."

Byron's eyes grew wide. "Why would you think that?"

"You insinuated I don't actually work because I'm wealthy. I thought you arranged for Eris to marry Jonathan so you could kill him and then talk her into giving you money whenever you needed it. When I found that button, I knew it couldn't be you because that thing is probably worth more than what you make in a year."

"The button isn't *that* expensive, but, as you pointed out, I can't afford it." His gaze went to Lord Hemmington. "He won't be out for much longer. Will you help me bind him up so he won't get away?"

With a nod, Charles hurried to help him. He could have told Byron about how he had suspected Eris of murdering Jonathan, but he thought better of it. At this point, it didn't matter what had caused him to marry her. He loved her. His marriage to her was the only good thing that had come out of his friend's death. He'd rather let everyone think he had loved her from the very beginning.

The important thing was that he'd been wrong about her.

He was very glad he'd been wrong.

And, better yet, he was finally assured that the person who did murder Jonathan wasn't going to get away with it.

***

Eris sat at her vanity and sipped some peppermint tea she'd had the maid bring up to her bedchamber while she was getting ready for the dinner party. Everyone in Charles' family was coming over this evening. She hoped she didn't say or do anything to make a bad impression.

She glanced at her reflection. She'd done all she could to look her best, but she wondered if it was enough. Just how did a gentleman's family judge the lady who'd only recently married into the family? Did they do it based on appearance, or was it the lady's disposition that mattered more?

A knock came at the door separating her bedchamber from Charles'.

"Come in," she called out before taking another sip of the tea. Her hands were trembling. If she had been smart, she would have asked for sherry. The tea was doing little to settle the butterflies in her stomach.

Charles opened the door and smiled at her. "You look lovely this evening."

She returned his smile. "Thank you. I hope I'll make a good impression."

"You have nothing to worry about." He went over to her and kissed the top of her head. "Of all the people in my family, I'm the hardest to please. If I think you're wonderful, they will, too. To be honest, I'm concerned about what you'll think of them. My younger sisters are too young to cause any problems, but my brother-in-law is a bit of a cad, and my sister has her scandalous qualities as well."

"I don't recall hearing anything about them in the past."

"That's because my father and I were careful to keep things quiet." He rolled his eyes. "I'll tell you about the time they got married after they leave tonight." He took the cup from her and placed it on the vanity. He helped her to her feet and kissed her. "They're going to love you. I can assure you of that because I couldn't help but fall in love with you. Having you with me has given me a lot of comfort after Jonathan's death."

She hugged him. "I'm glad for that, Charles."

He returned her hug and held her for several long moments. "I know you're not expecting yet, but I was thinking if we have a son, can we name him Jonathan?"

"Of course, we can."

He held her closer. "I never want to forget him."

"We won't. We'll keep his memory alive."

"I'm glad we're in this townhouse. I like being surrounded by the things he owned. Besides, this place is better than the one I used to own. I'm sure my father will be relieved to know I'll sell it to that gentleman he knows."

He kissed her then extended his arm to her. "If I don't get you down there soon, I'm afraid my family will come up here and drag you downstairs."

She accepted his arm and let him escort her out of the room.

"I have good news," he continued.

"What is that?"

"This evening we're really going to do those silhouettes you and Reina have been wanting to do for the longest time. We'll work on those after dinner, and since it's something we can all do, the ladies and gentlemen will stay together the entire night."

She did feel better knowing he wouldn't run off to another room with the gentlemen after dinner. While she was comfortable with Reina, she still had to get better acquainted with his mother and sisters.

"You probably won't have to do much talking," Charles said. "I'm sure Heather and her husband will spend half the time talking about their four-year-old son. Bridget and Melanie will tell you all about the games they like to play. I think all you really need to do is listen and nod."

"I can listen and nod."

They paused at the top of the steps and he kissed her cheek. “I did very well when I married you. There’s no one who would make a better wife than you.”

Her face flushed with pleasure as he led her down the stairs.

If you want to read about Heather's romance, it's already available.

Kidnapping the Viscount (Marriage by Fate Series: Book 5)

Miss Heather Duff met the love of her life. Then she let him go. And now she's determined to get him back.

If there's one thing Heather regrets, it's that she let Lord Powell go. She listened to other people tell her what to do, so when Lord Powell proposed, she said no. It was the worst mistake she's ever made, and now she's determined to prove to Lord Powell that she wants a second chance.

Gill Easton, Viscount Powell, has never stopped loving Miss Duff. But a gentleman has his pride to protect. He can't just let her walk back into his life as if nothing ever happened. And this puts him in a dilemma.

He'll have to resort to unusual methods in order to get the lady of his dreams to marry him. In this case, the unusual method is to convince her to kidnap him…without letting her know he's the one behind the whole scheme.

Don't miss this romantic comedy featuring a feisty heroine, a hero who has to play hard to get, a meddling brother who doesn't take even a minute to listen to what someone is trying to tell him, and a friend who doesn't mind any kind of scandal so long as the cause is true love.

Coming Next in the Marriage by Necessity series:

The Cursed Earl (Book 2)

Algernon Wright, Earl of Draconhawthshire, lives his life given over to superstitious ideas. His most pressing belief is that when he turns twenty-five, he'll suffer a grave injury and die. Being the remaining heir, he must conceive a son before his 25th birthday.

Miss Reina Livingstone doesn't believe in silly things like curses, but she fell in love with Algernon as soon as she met him. Since it means she can marry him, she offers to be the lady who can help him with his desire to get an heir, sure that, in time, he will come to love her and that they'll be together for a very long time.

I think this might be a romantic comedy.

Heiress of Misfortune (Book 3)

Mr. Byron Tumilson's job solving crimes has left him with little time for romance, which is why he had decided early on that he would always remain a bachelor. That all changes when he winds up in a scandal with the daughter of the gentleman who hired him to keep her safe so she could marry someone else.

You can join my email list to be notified as soon as these books come out by going to this link: https://ruthannnordinauthorblog.com/sign-up-for-email-list/

All Books by Ruth Ann Nordin
(Chronological Order)

Regencies

Marriage by Scandal Series
The Earl's Inconvenient Wife
A Most Unsuitable Earl
His Reluctant Lady
The Earl's Scandalous Wife

Marriage by Design Series
Breaking the Rules
Nobody's Fool
A Deceptive Wager

Standalone Regency
Her Counterfeit Husband (happens during A Most Unsuitable Earl)

Marriage by Deceit Series
The Earl's Secret Bargain
Love Lessons With the Duke
Ruined by the Earl
The Earl's Stolen Bride

Marriage by Arrangement Series
His Wicked Lady
Her Devilish Marquess
The Earl's Wallflower Bride

Marriage by Bargain Series
The Viscount's Runaway Bride
The Rake's Vow
Taming The Viscountess

If It Takes A Scandal

Marriage by Fate Series
The Reclusive Earl
Married In Haste
Make Believe Bride
The Perfect Duke
Kidnapping the Viscount

Marriage by Fairytale Series
The Marriage Contract
One Enchanted Evening
The Wedding Pact
Fairest of Them All
The Duke's Secluded Bride

Marriage by Necessity Series
A Perilous Marriage
Heiress of Misfortune – coming soon
The Cursed Earl – coming soon

Fairytale Regency Romance
An Earl In Time – coming soon

Historical Western Romances

Pioneer Series
Wagon Trail Bride
The Marriage Agreement
Groom For Hire
Forced Into Marriage

Nebraska Series

Her Heart's Desire
A Bride for Tom
A Husband for Margaret
Eye of the Beholder
The Wrong Husband
Shotgun Groom
To Have and To Hold
Forever Yours
His Redeeming Bride
Isaac's Decision

Misled Mail Order Brides Series
The Bride Price
The Rejected Groom
The Perfect Wife
The Imperfect Husband

Husbands for the Larson Sisters
Nelly's Mail Order Husband
Perfectly Matched
Suitable for Marriage – coming soon

Wyoming Series
The Outlaw's Bride
The Rancher's Bride
The Fugitive's Bride

Chance at Love Series
The Convenient Mail Order Bride
The Mistaken Mail Order Bride
The Accidental Mail Order Bride
The Bargain Mail Order Bride

Nebraska Prairie Series

The Purchased Bride
The Bride's Choice
Interview for a Wife – coming soon

South Dakota Series
Loving Eliza
Bid for a Bride
Bride of Second Chances

Montana Collection
Mitch's Win
Boaz's Wager
Patty's Gamble
Shane's Deal

Native American Romance Series
Restoring Hope
A Chance In Time
Brave Beginnings
Bound by Honor, Bound by Love

Virginia Series
An Unlikely Place for Love
The Cold Wife
An Inconvenient Marriage
Romancing Adrienne

Standalone Historical Western Romances
Falling In Love With Her Husband
Kent Ashton's Backstory
Catching Kent
His Convenient Wife
Meant To Be
The Mail Order Bride's Deception

Contemporary Romances

Omaha Series
With This Ring, I Thee Dread
What Nathan Wants
Just Good Friends

Across the Stars Series
Suddenly a Bride
Runaway Bride
His Abducted Bride

Standalone Contemporaries
Substitute Bride
Online Proposal

Thrillers

Return of the Aliens (Christian End-Times Novel)
Late One Night (flash fiction)
The Very True Legends of Ol' Man Wickleberry and his Demise - Ink Slingers' Anthology

Fantasies

Enchanted Galaxy Series
A Royal Engagement
Royal Hearts
The Royal Pursuit
Royal Heiress

Nonfiction

Writing Tips Series

11 Tips for New Writers

The Emotionally Engaging Character

Writing for Passion

Where to Find Ruth

There are several ways you can find me! I'll list them below, and you can pick the one that most interests you.

My Monthly Blog (https://ruthannnordinnewsletter.com) Once a month, I'll give updates on books I'm working on, and I will include new release information.

My Author Blog (https://ruthannnordinauthorblog.com/)
For anyone who would like to read my ramblings about books I'm working on, updates I'm making to books (such as new covers for boxsets), trivia about past books, and what my thoughts are in the writing and publishing world, this is the blog for you.

Keep updated on my new releases at these following sites:

(Click "follow" or "subscribe to author alerts" and Bookbub, Amazon, and Smashwords will send an email when I have a new book out.) The Email List requires a form.

Bookbub Profile Page: https://www.bookbub.com/authors/ruth-ann-nordin

Amazon Profile Page: amazon.com/author/ruthannnordin

Smashwords:
https://www.smashwords.com/profile/view/ruthannnordin

Email List (https://ruthannnordinauthorblog.com/sign-up-for-email-list/) If you want to receive an email only when I have a new book out, this is a good option. I never spam. MailChimp holds your emails, not me. I value people's privacy and time.

Ingram Content Group UK Ltd.
Milton Keynes UK
UKHW020648050623
422889UK00016B/1745